AF490120

Some of this book is kept as historically accurate as possible to a point. HOWEVER, this is a work of fiction. Names, Characters, and incidents either are the product of the author's imagination or are used fictitiously.

Other books by this author:

Zombie World: Fortress

Zombie World: Islands

Zombie World: Escape

Zombie World: Betrayal

Zombie World: Crossroads

Zombie World: Solstice

Jump the Net

Please visit our *Zombie World: the series* FACEBOOK page for updates on future books or to leave comments.

Cover Art by Rebecca Kaiser

The Past is Dead

By:

Michael Brown

Chapter One

Molly looked to the back corner of the bar with a mixture of disbelief and humor. The noise coming from the corner was a loud roar as the men carried on. There were ten of them. They were soldiers she was sure of it. Their 10 matching haircuts alone were enough to present a convincing argument. Add in the copious amount of alcohol the'd consumed in the last three hours and dearth of body fat all screamed warrior. This was not a military bar however. those were closer to the base. This was on the other side of Jacksonville and universally considered a bar for frat boys and townies.

Margaret smiled at Molly as she filled her tray with another round of beer and shots for the corner. Ten tall iced glasses, three pitchers of beer and ten shots of tequila made up the tray. Maragret couldn't help but express a twinge of jealousy on her face as she smiled back. Molly stuck her tongue out at her close friend as she made her way to the soldiers. Margaret smiled as she approached the men. They grew quiet and Made a point of making eye contact and smiling at her as she unloaded the tray. They graciously helped her with the empties, and her tray was now refilled for the trip to the bar. A five-dollar bill was tucked between two glasses before she could leave. "Thanks boys!" She made deep eye contact and a wink to the one holding the cash and "accidentally" popped her hip into his chest as she turned towards the bar.

A loud roar went up as the others started rubbing his head and giving him a hard time at the attention Molly had given him. She smiled wide and her cheeks flushed as she walked away. She had rolled the shorts a bit higher and tugged the neck of her shirt down when she saw them walk in. "Hey, girl, how much is that already?" Molly asked as she bounced up with her perky, blonde hair and cheerleader personality.

"Seventy bucks in tips so far; a five or a ten every time I bring them a tray. I love these guys, Margaret." She laughed. Margaret frowned at the sum. "I was worried that they'd only stick around for a couple of rounds, but you'd never know they've been at it for hours without stopping!"

"Well my table of boys is getting pissed at the ruckus and one is thinking of saying something. The women are embarrassed to be there but haven't left yet."

"That would be one huge mistake I think. Those boys look serious as hell, yeah they are partying hard but I feel like they're animals in a cage. They may be behind a locked door but they hold the key to the door and can open it whenever they want." Margaret looked back in a moment of concern.

The tall olive-skinned one reached his hand up and waved to Margaret to prepare another round. She smiled and waved back as the roar gained volume again. "Coin Challenge!" the rest of the bar heard loudly as all the men in the corner reached into their pocket. The sound of coins being slammed on the table was followed by shouts as they all pointed to the shortest of the men. Black hair stubble littered his head and muscles bulged from under the shirt that tried hard to contain them.

"1st Confederate Marines? I thought we weren't gonna make those?" Someone asked as they passed it around.

"I had to," the man laughed as others punched him in the arm.

"What the hell ever." One replied.

"Guess the Chief drinks on us for the rest of the night gentleman." A redheaded bear of a man stood and spoke. Margaret smiled as she checked the backside of the man out. She was single; he didn't wear a ring so she figured it was ok.

Molly slapped her ass, "stop that." The two laughed as Margaret turned to grab the filled tray for the third time in thirty minutes.

"Here, your turn to make some money."

"Seriously?"

"Of course, go get some tips. I am sure your frat boys won't tip as well." Margaret smiled back with a wink.

Molly walked the tray over and sat it on the edge of the table as two of the men stood to make room. As before they helped her unload and then reload the tray with empties, someone slipped a ten between the glasses. "Thank you, sir," she said to the man attached to the hand.

He smiled back and watched her as she walked away as he made his way to the bathrooms. She smiled at her friend as she pocketed the money. The whole bar got quiet suddenly as "You bitch!" was shouted from her table. Everyone turned to look as a twenty-something man in a red polo shirt and khaki pants stood and pulled on a woman's arm.

"You keep your eyes on our table, not that idiot." He shouted as he pulled his hand up and back.

The man tried to move his arm forward to slap the young woman but found he was unable. A meaty hand held his wrist tightly. "That would be a mistake, my friend." The shorter man said without emotion.

"Who the hell do you think you are," he spun to face the shorter man. His buddies looked up at the two and laughed.

"I am just a man concerned with the young lady's safety."

"Tyler?" a voice shouted from the corner.

"No worries, I got this." He shouted back at his friend. "Now, I suggest you apologize to the young lady and sit down." He suggested as he tightened his grip around the wrist.

"Go to…" Tyler loosened his grip, grabbed the back of the man's hand, twisted and applied pressure that sent the man's face onto the table with a wet "THUD". The other men at the table shot out of their chairs and stepped back. The women continued to sit but were unable to restraint their smiles.

"Now I believe I asked nicely, apologize please." He paused to look at the woman and wink as a smile appeared on her face.

"I'm sorry," the younger man squeaked out.

"Louder please, I don't believe she heard you." Tyler insisted with a slight renewal of pressure on the other man's wrist.

"I'm sorry," the man shouted after a squeal of pain.

"Excellent! Thank you, sir, for your cooperation. Have a nice day gentleman." Tyler offered to the men standing back from the table. He turned to the woman, "You and your girlfriends are welcome to join my friends and I if you wish." He smiled down as he shook her hand gently. He stood straight and headed back to the bathroom.

"Tom, no!" a female voice sounded as a bottle broke against the table's edge.

Tyler stopped and turned as his buddies all stood up from their chairs in the corner. The man whose face had just been introduced to the table only moments before now stood a few feet away with the top of a broken bottle in his hand.

"You son of a bitch," His eyes were failing at holding back his tears. His hand shook with rage as he pointed it at Tyler.

Tom's friends looked to the short man, standing firm, no fear on his face. Then to the corner, where nine others were making their way towards them. They all looked serious, no sign of the alcohol they had been inhaling, but a look of death on their faces.

Four of them grabbed Tom and began to pull him towards the door. "Ok, Tom fun's over. We're out of here buddy. This is not worth it, let it go."

Tom hesitated and tried to pull away when he heard his best friend whisper in his ear."

"Dude, these are not the men we wanna mess with. Take a second and think it through."

Tom took a hard look at his target, saw the look in his eyes and the fact his hands hung loosely at his side. This scared him at how relaxed the man was. He looked to his friends and saw the same relaxed looks and decided to live another day. He dropped the broken bottle and let his friends pull him out the front door.

"Well ladies, time to sit with the real men here." One spoke as they all stood, grabbed their drinks and made their way to the corner tables.

Margaret looked at Molly and smiled. "Well, that just sobered them up, better start filling trays." They both laughed as they started grabbing ice-cold glasses from the cooler in front of them.

Chapter Two

Major Mark Peterson squinted as the smoke from the bar-b-que hit his eyes. This was day two of their liberty, and as always he and his wife Amy were having the officers and their families over for a cook-out. Flipping the chicken and then the ribs, Peterson decided it was time for the sauce. He grabbed the bowl with the brush in it and began to slop the sauce over the meat. "Amy, we about ready?"

"Yes, I'll start putting the food out," Amy replied as she stepped inside the house with Ladonna Pike close behind.

Ladonna, wife of Captain Brian Pike II'll give you a hand.

"Thanks for the cookout Major," the tall thin blonde spoke as he approached.

"Dave, you're new, but you'll need to get used to this after extended exercises. It's a tradition that I started when I came here. Also, no ranks allowed. This is a chance for us to relax and spend some time together as family." Mark smiled at his 2nd lieutenant.

Mark flipped the meat one last time before he pulled them off the grill and piled it high on a platter. He walked over and set the tray on the long table. Amy and Ladonna had finished filling the table with side dishes.

"Dinner is served," Amy shouted, and chairs were immediately abandoned to form a line.

"One last dish," Mark proudly exclaimed as he set a large platter on the table. He pulled the tin foil off, letting the smoke and steam evaporate away to reveal a large beef brisket. "My friends, a Wagyu beef brisket." The blackened cut of meat stood proud as the smell of the wood smoke hung in the air.

"Major, isn't that expensive?" The lieutenant asked as his eyes softened from the smell coming from the brisket.

"One of the benefits of being in Japan, it is pricey but nowhere near as costly as if I tried to buy one in the States. Besides, I finally got the chance to use the smoker I had the motor pool guys help build. Enjoy!" He ordered. The sounds of conversation died and were replaced by a chorus of gulps, hums and approving grunts.

"Ah, the sounds of happy Marines," Amy laughed as she began to fill her own plate. Mark laughed and followed his wife in line. Amy moved to the wive's table as Mark joined the men's.

"Well, I think the south would have won if Lee would have pushed harder." Mark

heard as he set his plate down. Lieutenant
Jerry Brown was leading the topic. "If he
would have hit at least one of the flanks
on that first day, and then followed it up
with a second change on day two, he would
have pushed Meade's army back and overrun
them."

"The north was outnumbered three to
two on that first day," Pike interjected.
"They should have finished them off when
they had them on the run. Plus, Pickett's
charge failed because they failed to
properly support them with Southern
Artillery."

"I agree with you on that Brian,"
Brown agreed, "if you listen to Confederate
lore, the south had a special ops type unit
but they were never brought up to assist."

"I never read that Jerry."

"Hey, my master's thesis covered it.
You should read it Captain, you might like
it." Brown smiled as he took a bite from a
rib.

"It's quite good actually," Peterson
offered, "I didn't even know the boy could
read, let alone make a comprehensible
sentence when he first joined the cubes."
The men all laughed as Peterson slapped
Brown on the back. "According to family
rumors, my third great grandfather led that
unit."

Brown stopped mid-bite, "Wait, your
grandfather was Jonas Peterson?"

"Yes," Peterson's face became confused. "You didn't mention him in your paper."

"I found the name only twice and couldn't confirm his position."

"Interesting," Peterson spoke aloud as he took a bite, his mind raced to put pieces of legend together. "I am named after one of his two sons. My grandfather was Matthew, and his brother was Mark. Matthew lost a leg towards the end of the war. I could not find much about Mark in my research. Family legend has it he had a large tobacco plantation in southern Virginia before the war but any other documents were lost after."

"Well that's more than I knew, and I researched the hell out of it for my paper," Brown replied after swallowing a gulp of beer. "Now you've got me wondering if he served with his father."

Peterson ontemplated the thought of father and son serving together as his officers relived and discussed old battles, the civil war being a favorite topic among this group. Eating slowed as conversation picked up.

The wives and girlfriends at the next table smiled and shook their heads at their men. They continued to discuss cooking, clothes and how to cope with the time when the men were away. "The food is amazing Amy," Lisa Brown spoke as she wiped her face with a napkin.

"Thanks, Lisa, Mark knows how to work the grill."

Peterson leaned back in his chair, "honey it's a pit. Grills are for Air Force weenies to burn burgers on. "A chorus of "AMEN's" sounded from the gathered Marines as a smile flashed on Petersons face.

"I am so glad you continue to have these cook-outs. We should do this more when the men are away." Ladonna said after taking a drink from her beer. "Any ideas what's next?"

"Well as always, Mark doesn't tell me thanks to operational security, but I think somethings brewing."

"I guess we wait. Thank God women are more patient." They all laughed. As the food disappeared the men sat back and rubbed their stomachs. The discussion continued until someone decided to pull out a deck of cards. The men started with poker and the women drew teams and played euchre.

Mark stood and walked over and stood behind his wife. He rubbed her shoulders as the women talked about the Pike boys and their latest escapades. Of all his officers, only Brian and Ladonna had kids.

Although currently serving as 3rd Recon Battalion XO, Mark ws once part of a unit known as "the Cubes."   The Cubes deployed as part of the 3rd Marine Expeditionary Unit. The base elements came from the 3rd Marine Division, 3rd Recon Battalion. The triple combination made the nickname easy. As part of the 3rd Recon Battalion, Mark has been deployed to Iraq twice, and Afghanistan three times.

One Purple Heart, two Bronze Stars, and a combat action ribbon made up one of his three rows on his salad bar. Many members of the current 3rd Recon Battalion came from the Cubes, including most of the Delta Company's 3rd Platoon (DRP) Deep Recon Platoon.

Mark was five foot eight and a hundred and eighty pounds but he was strong as an ox. Mark's fitness reports always commented on his ability to make quick smart decisions in battle. One of the Bronze stars was given to him for making quick, smart decisions and saving a platoon of Marines in Kandahar when they were surrounded.

Peterson was taken back by a strong puff of wood smoke. His face became fixed with a slight smile as his mind drifted to the fight. Peterson watched out the side of the helicopter as dust was drifting in the air from the wind gusting from the West. His team received the call for help as they were returning from a recon mission; Mark was a captain at the time and leading the patrol. They decided to fast rope from the helicopter a mile from the scene. It was the closest they could find a wide-open space to allow it.

Twenty men slid down the ropes at an intersection and headed north. They encountered medium resistance from the buildings and quickly silenced it. Amazing what a few M-203 grenades will do when shot through a window, Mark smiled briefly. They found the platoon in a former medical clinic, over half of the Marines injured and five dead. He left six Marines guarding the street along their path into the clinic.

His Marines picked up the dead and injured that couldn't walk and headed out the back. Three Marines covered their escape and left a present of Claymore mines and tripwires inside. They made their way back down the street, killing forty insurgents that tried to stop them. Half a mile down the road they heard the explosions as someone found their tripwires. Staff Sergeant Travis Flint stopped and grabbed the detonator from his side pants pocket. "Fire in the hole," He screamed as he flipped the toggle switch up and depressed the red button under it. The building exploded a half-second later and the team felt the pressure wave from the blast.

"Used too much, as usual, Sarge!" A fellow Marine laughed as they started back down the road. They briefly looked back as the black smoke rose above the buildings. Two of his Marines got hit on the escape route, one in the leg and another in the shoulder. Mark picked up the Marine with the injured leg and carried him for the mile and a half it took to get to a landing zone. They exited the narrow street and entered a large open space created years before when a smart bomb took out four square blocks.

The Chinook landed and six Marines stepped out to cover his team as they carried the dead and injured aboard. They immediately took off with the ramp still down and took fire as they rose into the air. He remembered it had to be blind fire since the dual rotors kicked up an enormous amount of dust and sand. His first Lieutenant took a glancing round off his helmet and Mark thought he lost him, till he stood up and ran his hand over the gouge. He removed his helmet and kissed it before smiling back at Mark.

"Right honey," Amy's voice brought him back to the present.

He shook his head and smiled, "Sorry hun, what did you ask me?"

Amy laughed as she took a sip of white wine, "He was not with us ladies." She reached out and touched his arm before turning back to the women and continuing to tell some story that Mark toned out. He walked over and grabbed another beer and decided to go back and join the card game.

Chapter Three

     "Major Mark Peterson and Captain Brian
Pike, Reporting as requested General." Both
men saluted crisply as they stood before
the oak desk. Their green coats and
trousers were creased perfectly. General
Donaldson finished writing and returned a
salute, "As you were, sit down gentleman."

     Mark and Brian took a seat in front of
the desk in the high back armchairs, the
red leather squeaked slightly at the
movement. "I have bad news, I realize you
just got done with a training exercise but
I have special assignment for you and your
men, straight from the top. Not sure if you
been keeping up with politics back home but
national tensions are on a pace not seen
since the Civil War. The Political divide
between the major political parties rivals
that of the north and south. Add to this a
passionate, divided populace growing more
disillusioned and convinced that the
elected leaders no longer represent the
views of the general population. Even in
this climate POTUS is planning an extended
vacation at the Presidential Retreat at
Camp David. We have also been warned of a
credible threat from the FBI that local
militia units have threatened to interrupt

the vacation while the CIA says there has been an uptick in terrorist chatter about his vacation."

"To meet the threat at Camp David, the Joint Chief's have decided that members of the 3rd Recon Battalion HQ and an enhanced Force Recon Platoon (Scout and Interdiction) will be recalled from Okinawa to the US to meet up with a new Heavy Weapons Platoon from the 2nd Marine Recon Battalion, 2nd Marine Division, Camp Lejeune NC.   This Task Force is being deployed to the vicinity of Camp David to enhance POTUS Security in the face of the new threat." The General let it sink in for a moment before continuing. "Gentleman you are to be called Task Force Cubes." The General watched a smile cross both of the gathered officers' faces.

"Don't know if 2nd Battalion will like that?" Mark smiled wide.

"Let them argue with the NCA over that." Donaldson laughed. "Take a Recon and an Interdiction Squad with you. You will be supplemented by a Mortar Team and a Sniper Section from the 2nd Battalion. The standard Marine security forces are being tasked to close in security. They will allow you to run perimeter security and create a Rapid Response team in case someone tries anything stupid."

"Sounds good General. When do we leave?" Mark asked.

"You have three days. Pack for the mission. You will arrive five days before POTUS. This will give you time to learn the grounds, area and other members of your team. Dismissed gentleman, be safe. Semper Fi!"

"Oorah," The men saluted as they stood, before turning on their heels and exiting into the hallway. "

"Well, this should be fun." Brian laughed as they exited the office building. The sun made them blink a few times as it assaulted their eyes.

Brian hopped into the back of the open-air hum-vee as Mark got in the front. Sergeant Kenny Hayes already had the vehicle running. He was the Major's driver when back at base. "Our offices please Ken."

"Aye aye sir," the sergeant replied as he took off. His driving became sedated when the Major was in the vehicle but Mark knew him to have a lead foot when by himself. Sgt. Hayes had quite a record for speeding tickets while off base. Mark let his mind relax and enjoy the five-minute ride. The vehicle stopped a few times to allow platoons of Marines to run in front of them. The cadences were sung taking all three men back to another time in their beloved Marine Corps.

"I should be ok for the day Sergeant. Return to your unit and thanks."

"Aye aye sir, just call if you need me." The sergeant replied before driving off.

The two officers split apart as they entered the two-story brick building. "Morning Sergeant," Mark smiled at his secretary as he entered his office.

"Morning Sir," Sergeant Sally Dirksen replied as she stood to follow the Major. "You have three calls to return, here are the fitness reports for the last bivouac, and here is your coffee," She sat his Marine Corp mug on the table. "Two cream and no sugar, your wife made me promise to help you cut down on the sugar sir." Sally smiled as she turned around and closed the door as she exited.

Mark smiled to himself at his wife's concern before opening the bottom right drawer of his standard-issue, government desk. He pulled two yellow packages of sugar out and tore the tops off, pouring the contents into his coffee. He hated sugarless coffee. He took a sip as he read through the notes of each call and decided those could wait.

He quickly read through the reports, the current squad rosters seemed to be working out. He wasn't sure at first but Master Sergeant Tyler Evans told him to give the squad leaders a chance and it appears to have worked out. He decided to allow them to stay in their current spots during this deployment and reevaluate again after.

"Excuse me, sir," Mark looked up to find Brian at his door.

"Come in Brian, what's on your mind."

"I am slightly concerned sir. Our unit has already been deployed to combat zones four times in three years. I know we are the best but doesn't it seem like it's a bit much?" Brian asked as he took a seat.

"Well let's see," Mark sat back in his chair. "We have eleven members that speak a total of six different Arabic dialects, twenty Marines who speak Spanish, fourteen Master's degrees ranging from the civil war to psychology to criminal justice, countless Bachelor's degrees in all types of disciplines, four officers that graduated from West Point with dual majors in history and psychology and Chief Petty Officer that's one semester from finishing med school. So as I see it the Marines can send us to do security at the next Tar Heels pep rally, take over the nearest Taco Bell or deploy us to the combat zone in Iraq." Mark laughed as Brian broke into a smile.

"Yeah, I guess that makes sense, plus I hate Mexican food."

"Look at it this way, our deployments have been four months at the most, pointed missions and so far only slightly intense."

"Yeah, slightly intense," Brian laughed. "My ass still holds the scars from

the fight to retake that small village in
the North."

"Yeah, one bullet, four holes." "Mark
laughed, "ouch! Let's see what happens
after this mission and then we will revisit
the thought after we see what comes of it."

"Aye aye Major, sorry to bother you,"
Brian stood and walked out as Mark returned
to his reports. He finally got bored and
looked at the squad's itinerary for the
day. Mark stacked the reports and headed
out. "Going for a run, be back later."

"Aye aye, sir."

Mark walked out the back door of the
office having changed into his PT gear. He
walked the two blocks to 3rd platoons
barracks and was just in time to join in on
the stretching. Lieutenant Jerry Brown was
leading from the front and looked to the
Major. Mark waved him off and joined the
back of the pack. The Marines readied
themselves for the run with playful banter.

"Ok Marines, time for a little run,"
Jerry announced. "Right Face, double-time,
MARCH!" The Men took off and headed towards
the coast. The squad ran for twelve miles,
Mark's mind running through scenarios of
the upcoming deployment the whole time.

Chapter Four

The C-130 cargo plane landed at the 167 Airlift Wing in West Virginia. The Marines helped each other stand up as the rear ramp lowered revealing the dark cloud filled the night. "Four hops, man that's a long flight sitting in those cargo net seats." Captain Pike smiled as he tried to stretch the kinks out of his back.

"Agreed Brian," Mark spoke as he copied the stretches. Each man reached under the seats and grabbed their rucksacks and slung it over a shoulder before grabbing their personal weapons secured at the end of each row. The thirty men made their way down the ramp to the waiting buses that had moved up to within 100 yards of the plane.

Each man tossed his rucksack into the opened luggage doors. Once free of their burdens they gather a few feet away and made small talk. A few lit cigarettes or cigars as they waited for their next move. Mark motioned for his 2nd in command to join him near a hummer. As they approached a Major stepped out to meet them with a cell phone in his hand. He handed it to Major Peterson.

"Major Peterson," Mark spoke into the phone. "Yes sir," Mark replied after a brief pause. A few minutes passed before he spoke again. "Very good Sir we will be moving in twenty minutes." He finished and hit the "end" button.

"Orders?" Brian asked after taking a long swig from an offered water bottle.

"We have about an hour ride ahead. We will enter Camp David and proceed to the northwest corner of the property. The 2nd Battalion moved in their last night and set up our camp." Mark paused to take a drink from the bottle of water the Major handed him. "Grand total we will have 80 Marines. We are going to let the normal detail handle security up close as usual. We want to keep things looking like business as usual. This was a scheduled vacation for the President and his family. They arrive in two days. Major, can you show us the layout please?"

The accompanying Major unrolled a detailed map of the compound on the hood of the HUMVEE. It showed the placement of the new camp. "Gentlemen, your command tent is here," He pointed with two fingers. "Your personal tents here, and here. Here you can see the layout of the two-man tents for the teams. Your Command, Recon and Interdiction squads are being supplemented with one Mortar and one Sniper and one Interdiction squad from 2nd Battalion. You have your own communications guy and your Medic Chief Petty Officer Brown has requested two additional medics to join you." The three

officers looked at the map for a few more
seconds. "Thank you, Major. Let's get the
men loaded up Brian." Mark ordered as he
rolled up the map.

The Marines boarded the bus and headed
North from the airfield on WV-11. The night
was dark so they could not enjoy the
scenery but the small talk continued in
pockets. The darkness made their arrival as
low key as possible, not wanting to alert
anyone in the area of their presence.

The bus entered the compound after
being stopped by the guards and inspected.
The Marines grew silent as they approached
their drop off point. The bus stopped in a
parking lot and the men quickly stepped off
the bus. Game faces were starting to show
on the individual faces. Each man grabbed
his ruck and the Squad leaders form them
up. Major Peterson and his command staff
lead the march off into the woods.

The entered the makeshift camp and
were greeted by Lieutenant Dave Stevens.
"Sir, 2nd Battalion, Special detail
reporting sir." The man snapped off a crisp
salute.

"As you were Lieutenant," Mark replied
returning the salute. Let's show the men
were they will be sleeping and have the
commanders meet in the command tent in
fifteen."

"Aye aye sir," the man spoke the
orders out loudly to the gathered Marines
and started them off towards their tents.

Mark and Brian found their tents positioned at the corners of the command tent. Being an officer had its perks they both thought to themselves as they lifted the flap and walked in. The tents were a bit taller and longer than the enlisted. Each had a table and chair that set a few inches from their cots. The table held a battery-operated lantern, a notebook, and a few pens. Mark set his rucksack in the corner and laid his weapon on his cot. He then stripped off his load barring harness to the relief of his shoulders. Mark turned on his heels and headed to the command tent. He entered to find a large tent needing 4 sets of poles on each side to hold it up. A large table stood in the middle with a smaller table to the left in the corner. The corner table held the radio gear and the antenna wire snaked through a small hole in the roof. The opposite corner held another table with a coffee pot sitting on a propane burner and a stack of white metal cups nearby. He walked over and poured himself a cup as the officers began to arrive. A few grabbed their own cup of coffee before joining the others at the big table. Mark and Brian walked up and Mark set the rolled map on the table.

"Gentleman, welcome. First, let me introduce myself, I am Major Mark Peterson 3rd Recon Battalion. This is Captain Brian Pike, my XO." Brian nodded as he looked at the officers. "Chief Petty Officer Mike Brown, our medical team leader." The Chief acknowledged the men before Mark continued. "As you know this is a special detail ordered by the National Command Authority himself. We have good intelligence that a group of homegrown terrorists plans on trying to kidnap the president and/ or his family while they are here on vacation." Mark paused to let that sink in. "Now we are tasked to supplement the normal detail. They will continue to maintain their normal schedules and security details. We will have two quick response teams ready at all times. I want one from a Recon Squad and the other to Interdiction. A mortar team and sniper team will be ready in full gear here at the camp to respond to where ever they are needed. Each ready team will be posted within 500 yards of the compound but remain hidden well within the tree line. Again if someone is stupid enough to try and gain access we will bring the fear of God and the U.S. Marines down on them." Mark smiled as everyone gathered took in a deep breath of pride. Mark unrolled the map on the table and weighted the corners down with items already on the table, "Captain Pike will show you where the teams will be placed."

Brian stepped forward and filled the officers in as his hand glided over the map. "We will work in eight-hour shifts with check in every two hours. Pick your unit call signs and let me know what they are by noon tomorrow. You men from the 2nd have been here longer than us. Anything we need to know?"

Lieutenant Stevens stepped forward, "Gentleman there is a bear that wanders onto the compound occasionally but it is tagged. If it approaches we will be notified by the stationed detail so no one gets caught off guard. Also, we are expecting some weather in the next few days so have you men take their rain gear with them to their posts." He stepped back when finished.

Lieutenant Johansen the 3rd Battalion staff officer spoke, "The last thing we need is PETA in here bitching cause one of us came face-to-face with a bear when taking a piss and filled it full of lead." The men all laughed.

"Ok," Mark took the conversation back over as the laughter died down. "The president and his family arrive in two days. Only the president, his secret service detail and the normal Marine detail know we are here, and only the Marines know where we are staying. The secret service stays close to the house so they should not come anywhere near our teams." Mark could not help but yawn, having been on the move for over 36 hours making hops from Japan. The gathered officers smiled as all the newly arriving men yawned within a few seconds of their commander. "Ok, let's wrap this up for now. Brian will have team rotations set by 0800 and we start them at noon tomorrow. Might as well get the men used to it before the principals arrive." Mark smiled as the men turned to leave, a few pausing to stretch tired and sore muscles. "Oh, one more thing," Mark announced loudly. "We are officially called Task Force Cubes," he smiled. "Sorry to you men from the 2nd but we are now 3rd MEF, 3rd

Marine Division, 3rd Marine Battalion, Swift-Silent-Deadly."

    "OORAH!," the officers sounded off in unison before turning again to leave.

Chapter Five

The sun rose on the base camp for the sixth time since POTUS arrived. It played peek-a-boo with the dark storm clouds that were growing thicker as the day began. "Looks like we might get a little wet Major," Lieutenant Jerry Brown announced.

"Looks that way. Man, this will be the fourth day of rain since setting up this OP. How are we doing Jerry?"

"Good sir, Observation Posts one and two have nothing to report," Brown spoke.

"No sign of anyone in the neighborhood for now. I had the first squad check both escape routes again last night. The men are bored but staying frosty." Jerry and his squad had taken one of the night watches.

"Copy that, go get some sleep Lieutenant."

"Roger that sir." The man snapped a salute before he yawned and turned to head to his tent. He found the small one-man tent, more of a small tarp strung over a piece of 550 cord. It kept him dry and that was enough he smiled as he crawled inside. He fell asleep imagining the comfort the president and his close-in guard detail were enjoying as his men slept in tents.

Mark moved to the center of the command center and poured himself some coffee before heading to the radio table. "Anything on the radio Corporal?" asked as the steam rose from his cup and filled his nose with the sweet aroma every Marine enjoyed.

"Nothing sir, the radio is clear." The corporal stated without looking up. Mark patted the man on his shoulder and walked to the open flap of the tent.

A loud, long rumble sounded overhead. The men stopped as they could feel it in their bones.

"Wow, that's getting close." One man was overheard saying as the second rumble of thunder sounded. Captain Pike was sitting on the ground eating his breakfast when the rumbles made him stop and stand.

"That didn't sound good." He commented as he stood next to the Major. He turned quickly; all his men were within a few meters, except the observation posts, either in their tents or standing guard. A few exited their tents and looked up to the sky. The clouds had blotted out the sun and grown incredibly dark.

A lightning bolt flew across the sky, a dozen fingers spread out as the bolt traveled across the clouds. "Captain, pull the OP's in, get the men back here fast."

The Major ordered as two more bolts of lightning shot across the clouds and lit up the sky. A thunderclap followed close behind the lightning and made the men cover their ears for a moment.

"Wow, that actually hurt," One sergeant commented as Brian grabbed the radio to order the OP's to close down and double-time it back to base. He handed the handset to the Corporal, "Call the Marine security detail," he didn't get to finish the order as the detail called them.

"Get your men undercover, we are in for a hell of a storm, meteorology is worried it may turn into a tornado. We are hunkering down and staying undercover for now, out!" the radio blared as the men had to struggle to hear over the thunderclaps sounding overhead.

"Tighten down everything, double-time it Marines. We got a hell of a storm brewing here." Major Peterson ordered and the men rushed around and checked all the tents and equipment. "Get the men inside their tents, Captain, probably the safest place for them, have them pull their packs inside as well if they don't have them already."

"Copy that sir," Brian turned and barked the order. Men rushed to finish securing the gear and then headed to their tents. Brian watched as packs and gear was thrown inside followed by the Marines. They zipped the flaps tight and hunkered down to await Mother Nature's wrath.

The men from the Observation posts ran
into the camp and received the same orders.
They moved quickly to their respective
tents to join their comrades. Brian and
Mark watched as three lightning bolts came
in from different directions along with the
cloud, they joined in the middle and a bolt
of lightning shot down to earth and hit
just outside the perimeter of the camp.

The hair on their bodies stood up as a
slight electrical charge seemed to run
through them. The noise was deafening as
the bolt struck. "Guess we wait it out here
Major. I am not going out there now." Brian
smiled to try and cover the fear that was
creeping upon him. Bullets were one thing,
Mother Nature was another.

The world seemed to grow green as the
storm grew in intensity. More lightning
bolts danced across the sky, growing in
frequency. Every third or fourth would join
with others and strike near the camp. The
wind picked up and the tarp above them
danced on the currents. Both men moved near
the table with the maps and crouched down
in the middle of the tarp. Rain began in
force and fell almost horizontal, making it
halfway under the tarp. They began to get
soaked as more lightning struck. They could
feel the electricity in the air. The bolts
appeared as bright white-hot flashes and
they had to close their eyes to protect
them.

Both officers were knocked unconscious
as the ground only a few feet away exploded
from a lightning bolt. The concussion threw

them back and destroyed the radio in the corner. Steam rose briefly from the area as the water was superheated. The men hunkered in their tents were already unconscious, their bodies being assaulted by the electricity and pressure waves from the lightning and thunder. The tents strained at the cords holding them tight, as the winds blew through the encampment. Tree limbs began to fall as the winds separated them from their trunks. A bright green lightning bolt hit in the middle of the camp and sent out fingers along with the earth. The men were thrown a foot into the air. They bounced off the ground briefly before being launched back up. Three, then four, then ten green bolts encircled the camp. The glowing green lines melted into a large net covering the ground occupied by the Recon Marines.

It shot skyward, taking everything above it, with it. It left behind a large smoldering patch of bare earth.

Chapter Six

The smell of moldy canvas and campfires filled his nose, and his ears were filled with the sound of a flowing river. Major Peterson rolled onto his back; his body rebelled against the movement. He ached from head to toe. He had not been this sore since Recon training as a first lieutenant.

"Ugh," he heard from his right. "What the hell happened?" Captain Pike asked.

"I have never been through that bad of a storm." Mark said as he let his head drop to the right, "What the hell happened to your ACU's?" Brian's uniform was a collection of big grey, black and charcoal squares. It looked to be made of wool. Mark looked and found his own had changed as well. He sat up and looked around. His Boonie hat was now grey canvas also. The tarp was off white canvas and held to nearby trees by thick twisted rope. The sound of distant drums filled his ears.

The Marine's tents were the same off white canvas but looked to be made of two separate pieces. Several campfires flickered nearby. The table used for the radio was now wood; the legs were thick and gouged with deep cuts. The top had paper, held down by a couple of rocks and several pencils of different lengths. The two chairs were plain wooden folding chairs; the color faded with a couple of dark red stains on the back of one.

"What the…" Brian asked making Mark's head spin. A few feet from the makeshift cover stood four horses. The dark brown beasts stared at the two men as they finally stood. Thick rope tied them all between two trees. On the ground under the rope lay four thin black saddles with gold stirrups. Several more horses were tied up in pairs around the outside of the camp. Two wooden wagons, with wheels of wood, held together by a metal band, sat between two large tents.

"Where are the weapons crates?" Both men walked to the far edge of the tent. They had secured five watertight, weapons boxes. The black boxes had been replaced with five wooden crates. Brian moved the canvas tarp from on top and gasped. "Confederate States of America" was painted on the top. "Uh, Mark?"

Mark watched as several of his Marines crawled from their nearby tents. The look of confusion filled all their faces. When he reached his Major he saw the blood had drained from his face. "You ok Brian?"

"No, No sir I am not," Brian replied as he looked to see the men's uniforms had changed as well. They stretched their sore muscles upon exiting until they saw their fellow Marines. Mark then noticed they were on flat ground sparsely dotted with trees and not in the thick forest that surrounded the Camp David compound.

"Someone tell me what the hell is going on?" A Marine said as he exited his tent and stared at the rest.

Corporal Thompson had pulled his jacket off and spun it around, looking inside and out. He began to laugh, "What? Did they drug us somehow, take off our clothes and replace them with this junk." He laughed harder, "Nice one, whoever you are. Come on out and join in the laugh." His head began searching for whoever had pulled the practical joke of the century. "Well," he screamed. "Come on, show yourself!"

"Shut up Thompson," Sergeant Nick Brenner ordered.

"But Sarge," Thompson pleaded as he looked around more. "It's the only explanation…" The man moved closer to the river, an old brick bridge stood a hundred yards to the east.

"I said stow it, Corporal." He ordered again. Sergeant Nick Brenner looked to his officers who were just as confused as the rest.

"Brian get comm's up."

"Sir, my radio is missing, so is the satellite radio," Brian replied with a confused tone.

Mark closed his eyes for a moment as the men slowly gathered around the officers. When he opened them he decided to dispel reality to look around with an open mind.

All the men's clothes were similar. Black boots with thin soles. Woolen pants and overcoat, linen shirts and vests underneath. The irregular colors and patches of fabric meant that whatever happened got confused by the Digi-camo ACUs they had been wearing and made its best guess at period clothing.

His lieutenants had two horizontal bars on their grey wool collars. Brian's showed one large star and he had three smaller ones. His sergeants had red "V's" wrapped around their upper arms, while the corporals and lance corporals had the same two yellow "V's".

He reached around his waist, instead of the nylon webbed tactical belt and holster he had a thick black leather belt. His holster had changed from molded plastic to black leather with a small string of leather wrapped around the slide and secured to a button. The drop holster was secured with another piece of thin leather tied around his thigh. He still had the 9mm he was relieved to see. On his left side was two snap like hooks. He thought briefly and then remembered he should have a sword as an officer. In the corner of the tent, he found two swords, in their metal sheaths. His and Brian's he guessed as he gave his Captain a quick look and saw the same outfitting.

"Someone want to tell us what is going on?" Master Gunnery Sergeant Tyler Evans asked. "Where are we and what happened to our clothes?"

"Sir my electronics are gone, no radios, no GPS." Staff Sergeant William Sutton pulled up the sleeve of his coat. "My watch is gone as well. He slapped his pants and then his coat like he was searching for a lost item. He found a chain attached to a button. When he pulled on it, a pocket watch popped out of a small pocket on his vest. "William Tango Foxtrot?" He asked the air as he looked at the round, flat silver case. He pushed the top button and the face popped open.

Half the men began searching for their clothes, finding the same thing. Staff Sergeant Ken Hayes reached inside his coat and pulled out a brown pipe. "That was never there before."

"I got one to," he heard from several of the men as they checked their coats. They all pulled a folded brown leather case, inside was tobacco and a box of small wooden matches.

"Guess someone knew I liked the occasional cigar," one Corporal said as the men laughed briefly. The levity lasted only a moment before the confusion jumped back amongst them

A couple of the men ran to their tents
and pulled out their rucksacks. The fabric
had changed and it looked more like a
collection of bags than a formed backpack.
Where thin metal tubes had once given the
bag strength and structure, only wooden
dowels now appeared.

They brought the sacks to the tent and
began emptying them on the ground. Where
the camelback should be was a large three-
quart metal canteen with a cork. The cork
was attached to the canteen with a piece of
string. The socks were grey wool and the
skivvies made with linen and held a
drawstring top. They still had their
claymores, explosives, det-cord, and
detonators, however. On top of the packs
were strips of canvas to secure a bedroll.

The web gear was now canvas; the side
pouches were hard and square with a copper
turnkey to secure the flaps. All their
grenades were in a pouch instead of secured
within reach on the webbing itself. The
pouches held their magazines. Maps were
untreated yellow paper, not the laminated
kind they normally carried. Private Lee
grabbed a small cloth sack, it felt damp.
He gave it a smell and withdrew from the
odor. Instead of MRE's inside, he pulled a
few large hard crackers and some salted
pork wrapped in greased-paper.

Corporal Doug Engleman moved to a
large canvas tent with a stovepipe sticking
out the top. Inside he found a few tables
and chairs. Pewter plates sat in a stack on
the far table with trays of silverware

inside. A few metal bins held uncooked rice and corn, with full sacks standing in the corner. Bags labeled "C.S.A." lie on tables. Each labeled with its contents, corn, coffee, sugar, flour and more. He grabbed a medium-sized sack off the nearest table and lifted it to his nose. "Tobacco?" he asked out loud before opened the drawstring and confirming that's exactly what it held. He walked back outside, "Um guys, you will not believe this but that's a civil war cook tent. A little better stocked than I remember reading about but still…" The man held a bachelor degree in history and was one of many lovers of the civil war in his unit.

Corporal Thompson began laughing harder, "Seriously. So now we are to believe we have gone back to the Civil War. Man, this is too good." He laughed harder, ignoring the stern look of Sergeant Brenner.

The three-team medics had grabbed their backpacks and were a few feet from the group. The bags had changed just like the rest. The canvas was a darker grey and a lot smaller than their old ones. Chief Petty officer Michael Brown was the lead medic for the unit. He went through each pouch attached to the wooden frame. The other two confirmed his findings within their own packs. He stood and walked back to the Officers. "Sir," he asked as he pushed through some of the men.

"Yes Doc, what's up," Mark turned to look at the navy corpsman.

"It's good news, bad news kinda thing." That was his favorite way to start when it was more bad than good.

Mark and Brian both smiled briefly at how many times they had heard that phrase. "Ok, give it to me Chief."

"Good news, we still have most of our supplies. Bandages, cotton, sutures and all the soft goods are there. Wrapped in paper and not the sterile plastic we are used too. Bad news, we do not have any of the IV supplies anymore. Catheters, tubing, and fluids are gone." A few of the men grumbled quietly as he continued. "Good news, Morphine syrettes are still in the kits. We also have a good supply of grunt candy, anti-diarrhea pills and the like. They are in multiuse glass bottles instead of the two-pill single-use packs like we normally carry. I also have a bottle of Ipecac syrup and a bag of Epsom salts. Sir, we haven't used that stuff in 100 years."

Mark looked down for a moment as he rubbed his temples with both hands. "Anything else?"

"Yes sir, our supply of gator-aide is missing, and Dasky's box of candy bars has changed to just plain chocolate bars. Other than that we have our Mp-5's and 9mm pistols."

The men looked briefly at each other in panic before spreading out and rushing back to the tents. Each crawled inside and found their weapons. Gunny Evans found his

suppressed .308 and pulled it out. He
opened the chamber and found it loaded. He
kissed it on the side and swung it over his
shoulder as he held the sling. "Thank God,"
he smiled at the officers. "I didn't want
to lose my "Kate." The Marines soon
returned with their web gear and personal
weapons held close.

Sergeant Brian Fisher had his M-248
around his neck, the two hundred round box
of ammo secured to the left side. "I still
have my baby as well. Three wooden boxes of
ammo sit in my tent next to a bedroll." He
said with a mix of relief and confusion.

Sergeant Paul Davis and Corporal Jon
Pickleman returned. "Sir, both mortars made
it and we have three crates of rounds for
each."

"Ok, so we have weapons and ammo, but
the rest has either gone missing or been
replaced with Civil War period gear.
Anybody wanna try and explain this please?"
Major Peterson ordered as he looked to his
Marines.A few minutes passed before an
answer was given.

Lieutenant Jerry Brown stepped
forward, "Sir, Occam's Razor, Sir."

A corporal looked to his Lieutenant,
"Occam's Razor?"

"Huh," Lieutenant Johannsen looked at
the man. "Sorry, it's a scientific theory.
It states that all things being equal, the
simplest explanation is usually correct."

The Corporal nodded his head in thanks and looked back to his fellow Marines. Confusion still filled the air.

"So you're telling me that storm sent us back in time?" Captain Pike replied.

"Sir, it's the only explanation. Either that or Thompson is right and someone snuck in, drugged us, changed our clothes and gear, moved us a few miles and dropped us here without leaving a trace or any of our sentries catching them."

"Ok, let's suspend that question for now. How about we start with where are we now?" He looked to Captain Pike.

Corporal Thompson started laughing hysterically again. The men watched as he tore off his coat and then his shirt off. "We're in Oz. No wait, we are in Wonderland. Look Alice it's the teacup party!" The man fell to his knees laughing.

Sergeant Brenner walked up and hit him in the back of the head with his rifle butt. "I said stow it, Corporal." He said as the man fell forward on his face. Brenner turned and looked at his Major, "Sorry sir, I didn't think he was helping."

"Perfectly acceptable Sergeant, I was about to shoot him." The Major laughed to try and ease the tension.

"Well if these maps are right," Brian started unfolding the yellowed papers. It revealed a primitive map, hand-drawn and marked with pencil. He looked first to the map with the bigger landmarks. Then to a second that was more hills and fields. He finally rolled out a big map on the wooden table. His fingers traced over the maps as he looked up and back a few times. "Sir, again if this is correct, we are four miles Southwest of Gettysburg, Pennsylvania. Sir we are still in what in our time was Camp David. We are just outside of Emmetsburg."

The Marines grew silent as they looked with disbelief at the Captain. Lieutenant Brown stood next to the Captain. He studied the maps in the silence for a few minutes. "Sir, I have to agree with the Captain. This is right near Gettysburg, sir."

"Well, that answers that question. Now who knows when it is?" The men looked south as the rumble of cannon fire began in the distance.

Chapter Seven

The men had spread out, some sitting
on logs near the fires. Others were moving
around exploring the area nearby, the late
afternoon sun slowly disappearing in the
west. The three medics found the medical
tent and were inside. Enameled pans, large
knives, A couple of hand saws, and stacks
of white linen-covered four tables spread
around the inside. There were three narrow
wooden tables spread in the center. A fire
holding cauterizing irons of varying sizes
sat near the middle of the back wall.

Inside the medical tent and next to
the officer tent and cook tent sat several
large wooden barrels, filled with fresh
water. Several Marines had grabbed metal
coffee pots from the cooking area and a cup
of green coffee beans. First they placed
the beans in a frying pan and set it over a
fire. They moved the pan continuously as
the beans roasted and turned dark. Next
they ground the beans in the only grinder
they could find. The coffee pots, were
filled with water from the barrels and set
on top of the low fires near their tents.
The grounds were added slowly. The coffee
filtered through cheesecloth before being
drunk from blue enameled metal cups.

The men were still confused but they were trying to make the best of it until they could figure out what exactly had happened. The sweet smell of pipe tobacco hung in the air as a few decided to try the pipes they found in their coats. A few had found playing cards and some small card games broke out as well.

Major Peterson had called his officers to the mess tent and they sat around a large wooden table. Corporal Doug Engleman poured them all a cup of coffee before heading towards the back. He had enlisted a couple of others to help him prepare the meal for the unit. "This mess tent is not a traditional thing gentleman but I will do my best to make something edible," Engleman laughed before stepping away.

"So, we all agree we are back in the 1860s in Gettysburg, PA." The gather officers bobbed their heads in agreement.

"Doesn't make sense Major," Captain Pike offered. "But it's the only thing that makes sense."

"Agreed, but the bigger concern; we are the most heavily trained and equip unit in the CONFEDERATE army." He emphasized the point. "We are holding weapons that haven't even been dreamed of yet, with untold firepower at our disposal."

"True," Lieutenant Jerry Brown added. "The Northern army just started using cased bullets and lever-action rifles; and only in a few special units, like recon scouts and Calvary."

"So next obvious question, do we fight for the South IF and when asked?" Lieutenant Daniel Johannsen offered.

The officers grew quiet, some taking a sip of their coffee. Jerry Brown pulled out his pipe and filled it with tobacco, lighting it with a wooden match before he took a long drag. He let the smoke marinate in his mouth as some drifted out the corner. He inhaled, tipped his head back and blew smoke rings up towards the roof of the tent. "It does offer an interesting conundrum." He finally spoke.

"Let's hear your thoughts Lieutenant," Mark ordered.

"Well, I think we have all wondered what would happen if just one soldier went back in time with even one M-16 versus a musket. Add to that the fact we know the military and strategic blunders General Lee made at this very battle." Jerry took another long drag on his pipe. "We also know where every Union Troop is placed." Brown let that sink in for a moment. "What if we are the Special Operation unit we have heard about? What if we could talk the powers that be into finally using us?"

"We are talking about changing history gentleman." Captain Pike replied quickly. "This would change everything for the United States." His eyes caught the look from every other man at the table. Corporal

Engleman and the two others Marines stopped
and were looking at the officers. "Slavery
for one, think about all the things we take
for granted that were invented by a black
man. "Air conditioning, the lawnmower, hell
even the first heart transplant. Would
these things disappear if we do this?"

"Not just that," Mark offered, "but
the south would break from the north. It
would split the country in two. Jefferson
Davis had not wanted to take over the
North. He just wanted the South to be free
to live the life they wanted."

The men all turned as the sound of
horses approached. Three Confederate
soldiers appeared and rode up to the camp
before dismounting. A young Lieutenant
walked up and saluted. "Excuse me, Major,
Colonel Peterson requests your presence,
right away." The man lowered his arm after
Mark returned his salute.

"Captain, accompany me to the
commander's tent," Mark spoke. "Gentleman,"
he turned to the remaining officers. "Start
talking to the men; get their opinions on
our conversation." The gathered officers
stood and saluted as Mark and Brain walked
to their horses. Two sergeants heard the
exchange and had started saddling the
horses.

"Where did you learn to do that
Sergeant Sutton?" Mark asked with a smile,
as the man tightened the leather strap
around the horse's belly.

"My parents had horses, sir. They own a two hundred acre farm outside of Louisville, been riding horses all my life." The man smiled back as he tightened the belly strap down.

"Saddle a horse for yourself Sergeant; I want you to ride with us."

"Roger that sir," the man replied and quickly saddled a third horse for himself. Brian and Mark watched the younger man as he stepped into the stirrup and threw his leg over the horses back. They imitated his movements and made it into the saddle.

"Lieutenant?" Mark asked the messenger.

"Miller, Sir."

"Lieutenant Miller how far is it to the command tents."

"About two miles sir. You and your men were kept aways back off the line to try and remain undetected sir." The man said over his shoulder as he led the way.

Sergeant Sutton joined the two officers, "Relax sirs, loosen your legs and enjoy the ride. Get in sync with the horse's movements or you will pay for it in the morning." He spoke quietly so as not to alert the others that they had never ridden before.

"Thanks for the advice Bill," Brian replied as he relaxed his legs and settled into the saddle.

The path was starting to wear from what they assumed were constant rides back and forth between the command tent and their unit. The grass was about worn to bare earth in a few places. The trees were thick and the smell of pine filled the air. The setting sun's rays darted in between the treetops and the cottony clouds, making for quite a beautiful ride.

Once they relaxed, they actually enjoyed the ride. The horses were gentle and moved in a rhythm that they quickly got used to. The noise increased as they approached the command area. Men were moving about and there were plenty of horses nearby. The smells hit them next; campfires, horses, and the pungent smell of unwashed men filled their noses.

They exited the trees into a large clearing. The command center was set on a hilltop with hundreds of tents in the valley below. Three large tents with several smaller tents littered the top of the hill. A canvas tarp strung between poles sat in the middle and three gentlemen stood inside. The Lieutenant stopped a few yards short and dismounted. The two sergeants also dismounted and moved to hold the reigns for Mark and his men's horses.

They made their way to the tent and made a crisp salute at the officers inside. All three men recognized General Robert E

Lee at once. The man spoke without looking up from the maps he was studying. "Major Peterson, your father says you have a special unit of men and weapons you have been training."

Mark hesitated at the surreal nature of what the man had just said. He looked to the Colonel and saw a slight family resemblance. "Yes sir."

"Tell me about them," the man ordered.

"Well sir, I have eighty men and three medics."

"Medics?" Lee asked finally stopping to look at the three men.

"They are trained to treat wounds on the battlefield sir. They can treat the wounded during a battle, allowing some to even return to the fight. When at camp they act as doctors, they can clean and suture wounds, and treat a number of ailments."

"Interesting never heard of that being done. What if the soldier needs a limb amputated."

"Sir they are trained for that, but have avoided having to use that particular treatment so far."

"So they just wait till someone is injured and then run into the field of fire to treat them," a nearby Major asked with incredulity.

"No sir, they are armed as well. They fight if needed, and they use their weapons to protect the injured if the situation calls for it." Mark replied sharply, staring the Major in the eye. The man withered at his glare.

"Well, Colonel Peterson here speaks highly of you and your men. I am still not sure if I should bring you into this fight yet." General Lee proclaimed as he went back to the maps.

"Sir, may I ask the situation," Mark took a step forward to try and see the maps.

"Step forward gentleman," he ordered as Mark and Brian moved to watch his hand move around the maps. "We met General Meade's Army of the Potomac, right here," he pointed to a spot just outside of Gettysburg. "They were dug into this row of low ridges to the northwest of town. We hit hard with two large corps of soldiers from the north and sent them fleeing through the streets and into the hills just to the south."

Mark and Brian instantly knew today was July 1st, 1863. "Well that answers that question," he thought to himself."My scouts tell me the union troops are stretched out in a fishhook pattern. I will be sending an assault against their left flank. They will hit hard around Little Round Top and Peach Orchard."

"That's a solid plan for the day General, if I may say so sir," Mark added as his fingers traced over the map. "Where do you think my men and I will help the best?"

"Depending on how the battle tomorrow goes I may use them the day after. I want your men to set up a patrol to the southeast today. Keep an eye out in case they try to flank us. I will send for you tomorrow to decide what to do next Major." The man saluted to show Mark and his men they could leave. The three returned the salute and headed back to their horses.

"Anybody else a little surprised by this," Bill asked as they mounted the horses.

"A little, that's an understatement, Sarge. Unbelievable is more like it." Brian laughed as he pulled the reigns to the right and nudged the horse with his heels.

Mark took a couple of deep, raspy breaths, "I find your lack of faith disturbing," he spoke with a deep voice between the breaths.

The three men laughed as they rode down the trail back to camp. "Wow that's gonna be a great movie, I can't wait the hundred and ten years to see it," Brian replied with a laugh.

Chapter Eight

The sounds of the distant battlefield grew as the morning sun rose in the east. The men were all awake and gathered around the command tent. Most held a cup of coffee or smoked a pipe as they waited for the Major.

Mark walked from his personal tent, he walked a straight line to the command tent and the men parted to allow him access. "Gentleman," he said as he arrived. "We have a decision to make. It has to be unanimous as well." He turned as he spoke, making eye contact with the Marines he commanded. "For some unknown reason, we have been sent back in time. We have been placed at a turning point in America's history. We stand here in the uniform of the Confederate States of America, and we have been asked to fight for what we all know to be the losing side in this conflict. However, eighty men stand before me, holding more firepower than both sides of this fight combined." He saw a smile cross the faces of a few of his men.

"I know every man here, has at one time or another, wondered about this very scenario. What if," he paused "What if, is exactly what we need to decide? Do we fight, or do we run and hide? We all know what the south fought for. We all know what they will say when they see weapons in the hands of Jones and Davis here." He pointed to the only two black men in his unit. "How much fear will fill their hearts when they see what those two black men can do," the men laughed at the thought for a moment.

"I have spoken to the Officers, and we agree. We were sent here for a purpose. We also agree we have no idea what that purpose is," he smiled as he clapped a nearby sergeant on the shoulder. "We are here, we are in this place, and we think we should fight. We have no idea how we got here, and no idea how to get back home. We also have no intention of running like cowards from a fight we know we can win."

"Sir?" everyone turned to see Sargent O'Malley from the 2nd Battalions Interdiction unit with his hand raised.

"Yes, O'Malley?" Mark replied the smile fading from his face.

"Sir, I have a family at this battle fighting for the North. My great grandfathers from my dad's side of the family. They fought with the 2nd Maine at little big top."

"My family was here for the south," One faceless voice spoke out.

"I also have family fighting for the Union." Several of the Marines had family at this battle. Serving for a lot of these men was a family tradition.

"Gentlemen," Mark bellowed loudly and the men quieted down. "I also had family here for both sides actually. I am not saying this is an easy decision. However, we have been brought here by some force. The officers and I have no idea how we would get back to where we came from. Some of you corporals and sergeants are just starting to work on your college degrees. Most of the officers have one if not two pieces of parchment and military history is a big one we have all studied. The south just wants its own country." Mark paused before continuing. "I have no doubt we will win this battle. I also have no doubt it will change the direction this war was heading in before this battle. Leaders on both sides believed the winner of this battle would take the war but it lasted another 2 years before finished. Imagine the lives we can save by maybe stopping the war here?"

He paused again to let that thought sink in. "620,000 men died in the civil war. 8,000 at this battle alone with another 32,000 wounded. And remember that these soldiers don't have a team of medics to patch hem up. They usually end up having a limb sawed off without drugs to dull the pain. Then they took a hot iron and cauterized the wound." A couple of the Marines winced at the thought of a red hot piece of iron burning a cut closed. "These are some of the things the officers and I discussed late into the night to come to this decision. As Marines, we believe in saving lives through superior firepower. Well this is one of those moments. We can

60

end this war potentially here and now. If we decide to fight we will bring more firepower than any army of this time period has ever seen and do it with just 80 men."

"I will give you one hour to think it over. We meet back here at 0800 to decide." The men dispersed a few small groups gathered around the campfires. Men sat on upturned logs or stood by the fires. Quiet conversations ensued as a few of the marines lit pipes. A couple men headed off on their own to think in solitude. Staff Sargent DeCapo went and sat on a fallen tree next to the river. He pulled a skinny cigar from his coat and lit it with a wooden match. He took a deep drag as he watched a few leaves float by, carried along in the quick current of the river.

Mark stood just outside the command tent, pipe in hand. The sweet smell of the burning tobacco kissed his nose as he looked around at his men. "Tough choice," he thought to himself as he blew the smoke out and up into the soft breeze. These are tough and smart men, he knew, you can't make it in the Recon Marines without those two qualities. Brian appeared at his side, sipping on his cup of coffee.

"They will come to the right decision Mark," Brian spoke softly after a sip. "Each man just needs to work out the details."

"Yeah, we had a few hours of discussion; they have an hour or so. A lot to think about, I am sure none of us have

all the details either. We will change
history with what we can do here." Mark
finished as he hit the pipe again.

"Then what?" Brian asked.

"Honestly? I have no idea, we cross
that bridge when we get to it." Mark
replied as he looked sideways at his second
in command. The two men continued to stand
at the tent flaps in silence as first the
officers then finally the men began to
gather inside. Mark waited another ten
minutes as the last of the men arrived
late.

Mark turned from the opening and moved
closer to the men before beginning.
"Gentlemen, we have all had time to think
this through. I will be honest I don't know
what comes after this. Some of us may die
in the fight. To think we won't just
because we have superior firepower is
foolish. As I said before we stand before a
chance as we have only dreamed of. We have
been given a chance to change history."
Mark walked and clapped his hand down on a
few of the men's shoulders.

"Men of the 3rd Battalion," he spoke
louder. "We wear the uniform of the Army of
the Confederate States of America. We have
been asked by General Robert E Lee to fight
for that Army. History has shown us that a
special unit DID exist at this time and
that they were close to the battle.
However, the General decided not to use
them. Well we are here now, we ARE that
unit." He paused to return a smile to the

faces now starting to show their own smiles. "We have a choice to make and it must be unanimous." Mark stood in between the open flaps of the tent, the sun shining brightly behind him, silhouetting him to the men. "So, what say you, men of the third platoon, of the third battalion, of the third Marine Division? What say the Cubes?"

All the men raised their hands at once; "We fight!" was the cry, loud and proud. "Fight, fight, fight," the cheer was chanted by all present.

"Right," Mark shouted after letting the men get completely fired up. "Leuitenant Brown," He shouted as the men quieted down.

"Sir," Lieutenant Jerry Brown stepped forward into the inner circle created by the men.

"Take first Recon squad along with a sniper unit and mortar team one, set up to the Northwest. Keep an eye out for a flanking maneuver from the blue bellies." Mark added the confederate term given to the Union soldier. "Here is where I want your team Lieutenant," he showed the man on the map.

"Aye aye Major," Jerry turned, pocketing the small piece of yellowed paper. "Marines, you heard the man, weapons and ammo, you got three minutes. Let's move people!" He shouted as he moved to his tent. Jerry returned in two minutes, his sword by his side and his rifle over his shoulder. The men gathered shortly after him, weapons and ammo ready for the hike. "Ok squad let's move out. We move one mile and set up an ambush site. Corporal Jones, you have point." He ordered and the men moved out.

"Give me a three-man Observation post to the northeast. Wild Bill, take Fisher with his sixty and Lamont to assist." After his ability with horses, Mark had chosen the man's new nickname. He handed a small map to the man to show him where to set the O.P. up.

"Roger that Major," Wild Bill Sutton replied as he nodded at the two men joining him. They grabbed their gear and moved off. "Captain Pike send a man with each unit to act as a runner, and give me two more here in case."

"Copy that," Brian replied as he taped four men standing nearby. They ran to grab their weapons and catch up with the units they were assigned to.

"The rest of you," Mark turned to the remaining squads. "Take turns stripping and cleaning your weapons. Relax, we shall be in this war soon enough." Mark moved to the map table as the remaining men dispersed. They seemed almost happy to go to war in this situation.

"Nice speech Major," Brian smiled returning to the command tent.

"Had to say something Brian," Mark smiled back before marking his unit's positions on the map. "What am I missing Brian."

"Nothing yet sir; we don't know what will happen if and when we start shooting."

"The rate of fire we can bring down is gonna scare the hell out of the union, that I can guarantee." He smiled briefly. "DOC!" he shouted.

"Doc" Brown ran up from the medical tent. "Yes sir," the man snapped to attention.

"At ease, Chief," Mark stood to look at the man. "How you set Doc."

"Sir I have a large pile of sand behind the tent to soak up blood, a box of large knives and saws, and a pile of linen to use for bandages. Thank god I have most of our medical gear, sir. The only medicine I can find is Epsom salts, some form of liquid opium, and syrup of ipecac in the medical tent. I believe the opium is what they used to call, laudanum. It is effective and highly addictive. I will use it if needed but I prefer our meds as a first-line."

"Why not use their supplies first," Brian asked.

"Sir the bottle says opium, not how much in what concentration. It would be guessing if I gave the men any dose. I prefer not to "titrate to effect" as it were, with an unknown narcotic sir." The man replied with a serious tone.

"Ok, Mike, you're the doc. You do what you do best. Dismissed," Mark saluted as the navy corpsman ran back to his tent.

Chapter Nine

    Lieutenant Brown and his men had set
up a few feet from the markings on the map.
They found a few trees that had fallen and
stacked them, creating a nice camouflaged
and protective barrier to ambush from. The
twenty men made three areas, twenty feet
apart.

    They set up the mortar team in the
middle, with a sniper on the right side for
protection. The right foxhole held an m-60,
his assistant gunner and four men with m-
16s. One held an m-203 grenade launcher
underneath. One on the left was Jerry's
command center. He had four men with him
and their rifles.

    Once set, Jerry had six claymores
placed in a funnel created by the trees. He
figured if they came it would be from that
direction. The detonators were resting in
front of him on the limb of a downed tree.

    The men relaxed as the tasks were
done. The sun slid overhead as the hours
passed. The distant sounds of a battle
could be heard with the occasional birds
chirping from the trees. The men would
occasionally pull the cork from their
wooden canteens and take a gulp of water or
pull a piece of beef jerky from their

pockets, cut a chunk off with a knife and eat it. Sergeant Travis Flint, the team's sniper, turned and sat with his back to the trees after scoping the landscape with his rifle for the umpteenth time. "My great, great grandfather fought here." He said as he took a drink from his canteen, stopping to pour a little over his brown hair.

"Seriously," Sargent Tim Goodman replied, still looking around with the brass and wooden set of binoculars he carried.

"Yup, he was a Captain in the Union Calvary. I have a picture of him back home. Got it from my grandfather when I graduated from recruit training." He pulled a piece of jerky from his backpack and took a bite. "He was an amazing man, I am told. Grandpa said he was wounded twice, once here and later in Virginia, just before Lee surrendered. He met his wife when he returned home to Connecticut, married and popped out six kids." He smiled as he looked at the five-man mortar team listening.

"He made his living as a blacksmith. He was one of the best, made the gates for the fence that surrounds the Governor's mansion, still there I understand. He bought one hundred acres and his kids helped on the farm. Grew wheat and corn, raised cattle, pigs and chickens, even made his own whiskey," the younger man smiled. "He taught my great grandfather how to be a blacksmith. Great Grandpa fought in the army against the Mexicans in the early part of the century, lost his leg as a matter of fact. He and granny had eight kids, all girls except for my grandpa. Man, you should hear the stories he tells about growing up in "Estrogen Ocean", as he calls it." The men had a laugh as they could not help but be sucked into the tale. "Grandpa was too young for the First World War, but he made it into the second. He was too old to fight on the lines so he taught Marines how to shoot. Man he could hit a squirrel running from fifty feet with a three dollar pistol," he smiled as he drew the men in more.

"His first wife died from consumption shortly after the end of the war. He remarried a few years later to a woman much younger than he was. Apparently, my grandpa held his age well." He smiled as the thought of him and grandma raced through his mind. "They had my father and three other children before grandpa died at the age of eighty-eight."

"Grandma sold the farm they had and moved to Boston. Dad got a job when he was fourteen working at a grocery store, and then a factory at the age of seventeen. He joined the Navy in 1968 and served as gunners mate on the U.S.S. Missouri. Man, I loved listening to the stories of those big guns firing. "Would rock the boat" he always said. He served in Vietnam for two tours before mustering out and coming home. He stayed near San Francisco and met mom. They followed family tradition and had five kids. My one brother joined the Navy, my three sisters joined the Air Force, Coast

Guard, and Army, so that meant I had to
join the Corp." The men shook their heads
at the humor of the moment. "It's ok; I
love what I do, and who I do it with. I
pick on my brother; call him my chauffeur,
God how that pisses him off." The sniper
smiled for a moment before he began to
frown. "Guess I won't be seeing any of them
again." The rest of the men took a somber
pause as the reality of never seeing
friends or family again hit home.

"Psst, heads up, movement." Lieutenant
Brown called out quietly as the men turned
and prepared for a fight.

Sergeant Flint brought the rifle to
his shoulder as he spotted a man on
horseback. He looked through his scope and
saw the blue coat. "Union Calvary," he said
quietly. "I call it six hundred yards."

"Agreed Sarge," Sargent Goodman
replied. "He's all yours."

The Sergeant pulled the rifle tight to
his shoulder. "Weapons free," he heard the
Lieutenant say and he snapped the safety
off. A breeze kicked up and blew his hair
to the right. He took his left hand and
made an adjustment for the wind on his
scope. Flint slowly pulled his finger back;
taking a deep breath, he held it for a
second as his heart rate dropped. He slowly
let the air out as he finished putting the
three pounds of pressure on the trigger.
The crisp snap of the trigger told him he
had fired before the pressure on his
shoulder increased briefly. The suppressor

quieted the report of the rifle to the
point it didn't hurt anyone's ears.

The sergeant watched as the man on
horseback was thrown by the impact of the
bullet against his chest. Sergeant Flint
disappeared in front of the rest of the
men.

"Open Fire!" Lieutenant Brown
announced and the mortar team fired the
first round downrange. It exploded among a
group of three horses, killing them and
their riders instantly. They fired three
more before they looked to see two of their
team frozen in fear. The men stared at the
space the sniper once occupied. "Hey, get
your head out, we got a fight on our
hands!' The Sergeant in charge of mortar
team one ordered.

"Sir, Flint… He just…Disappeared…" The
men could barely speak as Sergeant Patton
looked and saw the empty ground. Only his
backpack sat where he once did. "What the…"
A musket ball flew past his head and
brought him back to reality.

The automatic gunfire to the right and
left filled their ears as they re-adjusted
the mortar. Horses ran fast into the
gunfire, flanked by infantry. The Union
soldiers screamed as they ran, bayonets
attached to the ends of the long rifles.

"Kill box full," Brown shouted as he
and the two men with him rapidly slammed
their hands on the detonators three times.
The claymores exploded almost in unison,

filling the area in front of them with ball
bearings. Men and beasts turned into
hamburger in the deadly arch of fire. A
pink mist hung in the air as the Union
soldiers behind them stopped. They turned
rapidly and retreated, dropping their
weapons, hoping to not be shot as they
fled.

     The area grew silent as the screams of
the scared soldiers died. Jerry stood and
glassed the area with his binoculars. "Nice
job Marines, they are running home to
momma." He laughed as he turned to see the
men in the middle foxhole staring at each
other. Jerry ran over, "Wounded."

     "Negative sir, its Sergeant Flint
sir."

     "What happened, where is he?"

     "That's just it sir. He just
disappeared."

     "How does someone just vanish
Sergeant," Jerry asked with a mix of anger
and confusion.

     "Sir I don't know sir. He was telling
us about his grandfather that fought here.
We saw the soldier on the horse; he shot
him and then disappeared. He just vanished
in thin air, his weapon too."

     "Oh shit, we have a problem I didn't
expect. Ok, break camp. I think we scared
the hell out of the enemy enough to keep
them away for the night. Police up

everything you can and let's head back to camp." Lieutenant Brown went back to his foxhole to grab his gear.

"Sir, I am not finding any brass," one of the men told him as he placed his empty magazine back into the pouch it came from.

Jerry looked around; he also did not see one brass casing on the ground. It should be littered with them he thought.

"Sir," Sergeant Lamont on the M-60 shouted. "I don't have any spent brass or belt links either.

Jerry pointed his weapon at a tree down range and fired off three quick shots. He watched as the brass was ejected and then vanished before hitting the ground. "What in the name…" He turned to see the disbelieving stares of the men. "Ok, let's go. We gotta report this to the Major, fast!" He ordered as the men grabbed the gear and began to run back Southeast.

Chapter Ten

Major Thomas Buchanan of the V Corp's
Calvary rode his horse hard. The Major and
his mount breathing fast. He hadn't noticed
he lost his hat a mile back. He rode up to
the command tents and found Major General
Henry Slocum sitting in his canvas sling
chair next to a table covered in maps.

The soldiers on guard duty lifted
their rifles and began to look around. They
figure he must be being followed if he was
riding so fast. The Major yanked on the
horse's reins and it skidded to a stop as
he jumped off, just dropping the reins.

He ran the last twenty feet before
quickly firing off a salute and then
bending at the waist, totally out of
breath.

"Major, calm down, what in tarnation
has you so worked up," the general asked as
he pulled out a cigar. He listened to the
man cough a few times as his breathing
finally began to slow. The General grabbed
a stick from the nearby fire and lit his
cigar with the burning end. He took a
couple of deep pulls from the cigar as the
Major finally was able to stand upright and
breathe normally. The general could not

believe the intense look of fear in the
man's eyes.

"Sir, we did as you asked, I took two
squads and headed down our right flank. We
found an open area that looked like a good
spot to set up a lookout and decided to
head down it. The grey backs were there
first." He coughed as a Lieutenant offered
him a canteen. He took a sip and coughed a
few times before taking a deeper pull.
"Colonel Flint was ordering his men when
his chest exploded. He fell off his horse
and we never heard the shot. Seconds later
the far end of the draw exploded in
gunfire. Sir I have never heard that many
rifles fire that fast. It was unbelievable
Sir. It sounded like a steady stream of
gunfire as the men ran into it. There were
explosions all around us but no cannon fire
to account for it." The gathered officers
looked to each other with a mix of fear and
disbelief.

"Fifty men on horseback and another
fifty on foot ran headlong into the
gunfire, firing blindly. I got a late start
and was about one hundred feet behind them
when the trees on both sides seem to
explode. It killed every last man and horse
in front of me. There was a cloud of blood
that hung in the air as the smoke rose up.
They had been blasted to bits, Sir. Parts
of man and beast lie mingled in the dirt."
The man took another drink to wash down the
vomit that rose in his throat from the
sight as he remembered it. "I caught a
glimpse of maybe twenty to twenty-five men

in three fire positions further down," he
continued after a moment.

"I pulled hard on the horse and high
tailed it back here sir. I have no idea
what truly happened but I have never seen
nor heard of that much firepower sir."

The General stood and walked towards
the man. He looked hard into the man's
face. Sweat continued to pour from his brow
and his body shook as the General placed
his hand on his shoulder. "Ok Tom, relax
you're ok. But we need to get this
information to General Meade as quickly as
we can." He turned rapidly, "Sergeant, get
my horse, and get a fresh one for the
Major. Colonel Daniels and Stevenson you
get the word out to the men to hold fast
until further orders.

The two officers rode with three
soldiers following close behind. The Major
was finally starting to relax the further
from the front he got. He knew they were
close to General Meade's command post as
they past lines of soldiers dug in. As
horses approached they saw General Meade
standing with fifteen other officers, his
hand moving rapidly above a map.

The two officers dismounted and handed
the reins to the soldiers that had
accompanied them. The gathered officers
stopped and looked up. "General, what's the
word from your flank," General Meade asked.

"General we may have a problem, sir,"
The man spoke in a serious tone as he

motioned for Major Buchanan to tell his
tale again. The Major spoke for five
uninterrupted minutes as the high command
tent officers looked around with the same
fear and disbelief as General Slocum's
staff had.

"Major, how many of your men
survived," a Colonel asked breaking the
silence.

"Sir, only ten men, including myself
made it out of there."

"It sounds like General Lee got his
hands on some of our Gatling guns," General
Meade spoke out loud what he was thinking.

"Sir," a major quickly spoke. "That's
impossible, Sir. They have only been in use
for less than a year. And all of those made
are accounted for. Even the ones sent to be
used in battle. As you know any unit with
one has explosives and orders to destroy
the Gatling gun at all cost if they think
they might fall into Confederate hands."

"Excuse me Sir, but I have heard those
fire," Major Buchanan interjected. "These
were not Gatling Guns. These fired in rapid
bursts, much faster than the methodical
Gatling. Plus when I got the look at the
firing positions there was no horse to tow
the guns and nothing resembling a cannon
either sir. I only saw handheld rifles, and
even those didn't look like the standard
Confederate muskets."

General Meade grabbed a glass of whiskey from the edge of the table and walked a few feet away from the tent. He looked out onto the small open field in front of him and the mass of tents that had been erected for his men. He watched as wounded were being brought in by wagon to the hospital tents on the right side of the camp. He took a sip from his glass. The injured men were pulled off on liters and taken inside. He watched some writhing in pain and could see the blood that stained their wool clothes at the point of injury. He was thankful their screams of pain did not reach this far. It had already been a bloody battle and it was only day two.

"How could the South have developed such weapons and he heard nothing," he thought to himself as he changed his gaze to the men marching back into camp from the far end. Those returning looked tired but not beaten. "Morale was high, but what if word got out about these new weapons?" He thought more as he slowly sipped from the warm whiskey. His staff looked on, knowing not to disturb the General when he was this deep in his thoughts. "The boys from Maine gave the grey backs a walloping today and held the flank," he continued to run today's battles through his mind.

Finally, he finished his glass and turned to walk back. "Gentleman," he stood in front of Major Buchanan and General McMurtie. "You will repeat this to no one. Inform your staff to not speak of it either, this kind of news if not confirmed could kill the spirit of the men." He

turned to his staff, "I want scouts sent
out to confirm or deny that the south has a
special unit of new weapons as soon as
possible."

The Colonel he stared at quickly
turned, "Runner," he shouted as he walked
away.

"Next, return to your area and I will
bolster your men with Major White's
Calvary. Hold our right flank tomorrow,
that's an order."

"Yes Sir," the two men replied with a
crisp salute as they motioned for their
horses. They quickly mounted and rode off.

"I want a rider to head to General
Hooker's army and warn him of possible new
weapons and tactics by the South but
nothing specific. I don't want to panic
them but they need to be aware. And maybe
they have heard of the same thing in their
area of battle."

Chapter Eleven

All the Marines stood and walked towards the returning squad. "How'd it go boys?" "Well did they taste the power?" these questions soon stopped as they realized they were short a man. Then the looks on the faces told them more.

Lieutenant Brown walked up to Major Peterson and Captain Pike. He saluted quickly. "At ease, Jerry. Report?"

"Sir we found a nice grove of trees and set up one hell of an ambush." He took a swig from an offered canteen before replacing the cork and continuing. "Nice open V-shaped area, six claymores, 3 firing positions. We sat for about five hours; Sgt. Flint was telling us how his great, great grandfather fought here when a mixed group arrived. I would say half Calvary and have infantry. Flint sighted in the Officer, easy shot, 600 yards. We all watched the man's chest take the hit. As he fell I ordered the men to fire and we unleashed hell on the 100 or so soldiers." Brown paused again to take another drink, this time it was a shot of whiskey offered by Captain Pike.

The rest of the men had gathered to listen and the returning soldiers shucked their packs and sat them at their feet. The smell of tobacco filled the air as smoke rose from a few cigars and pipes lit while listening to the report.

"Thank you, sir," Jerry offered as he returned the flask to the Captain. The enemy saw us and charged right into the kill zone. We used three motors shells before we set off the claymores. That finished the fight right away. It vaporized man and beast. Those remaining turned and ran for dear life. Some dropped their rifles others just hauled ass, sir."

"CUBES!" a shout went out with a small roar of agreement.

Major Peterson raised his hands with a smile to calm the men. He was sure the bad news was coming. "Continue Lieutenant."

When the enemy was gone I ordered the men to police the area for brass and prepare to move. I turned and Sgt. Flint was gone."

"What do you mean gone?" Captain Pike asked.

"Sgt Patton?" Jerry stepped aside to let the man forward.

"Sir, Flint shot the officer and then he disappeared sir. Nothing left but his pack." The Sargent handed the Major the pack.

"Oh shit," Mark muttered under his breath.

"Sir one other thing," LT. Brown moved back to the front. "We have no spent casings." He spoke deadpan.

"What?" a member of the group spoke.

"Sir, May I?" he motioned to his weapon.

"Of course," Mark replied as the LT. had the group open a lane towards a large tree. He lifted his weapon and fired a quick three rounds at the tree. All three hit the same spot, sending bark in all directions. The men gasped as the three casings sparkled for a second as they caught the sunlight and then disappeared before hitting the ground.

The group fell silent in disbelief. "How is this possible?" One of the men asked.

"Sir, I think I have some sort of explanation." Lt. Brown offered.

"You have the floor, Jerry. Please go on." Mark replied, the look of disbelief and confusion filling his face just like the rest of the men.

"Sir, first, I think Flint shot his great, great grandfather. When he did this he changed his own future, making it impossible for him to be here. So he just disappeared like he never existed. Next, since the brass casing has not been invented yet, once it leaves the weapon, it also doesn't exist."

"So you mean to tell me once we use the ammo we have no way of reloading the brass?" Sgt Lamont asked above the officers.

"Exactly, we have the ammo we have I think."

Patton pulled the spent magazine out of his pouch. "This is the one I…" his voice trailed off as he lifted the magazine only to find it filled again. "Um, sir?" He looked to Brown with even more confusion. The rest of the detail pulled their spent mag's only to find them filled.

"Ok, now I am totally confused." Lt. Brown spoke. "This makes zero sense. " Tom, check your mortar rounds. The Corporal ran to his tent where the three wooden ammo boxes that held his spare rounds sat. He lifted the cover on all three, knowing one full case should be empty since they took the rounds with them.

"Sir, all rounds present and accounted for sir?" He spoke matter-of-factly, before returning to the gathering. The marines began to grumble and ask the same questions out loud he was asking himself.

"Ok," Peterson spoke loudly after a few minutes. "We all knew this was going to get weirder. We can't explain how we got here. We decided whatever brought us got

confused by our camo and gear. So this is
just another thing that it's not sure how
to handle. So good news, we have ammo and
will not run out apparently." Mark took a
moment to lite his pipe and took a long
pull before continuing. "It's the Flint
thing that bothers me more." He paced
around the command tent for a moment.
"Gentleman, we all knew we were about to
change history when we voted to fight. Some
of us have family fighting on both sides.
So whatever our actions from this point we
have already started down that path. The
Northern Army has been told of the ambush
by now. They most likely will be confused
by the story of massive firepower and our
rate of fire we brought down on them."

Mark took another mouth full of smoke
before continuing. "So do we continue to
fight?" He stopped and looked at the men.
"We will most likely be asked to help
tomorrow. That's Pickett's charge remember.
We know what they did wrong. We can change
the tone of the fight just with a few
rifles and mortar fire. But by doing this
we will massively change history. Our
actions will put the fear of God into the
soldiers and officers of both armies." He
smiled around the pipe for effect. "I
cannot say we won't all just disappear in a
silent moment as we decimate the men from
the north. And I have no idea what happens
after the battle. What I do know, is you
are the best group of fighters it's been my
sorry ass privilege to serve with. I can't
help but smile at the thought of the looks
on the faces of both armies as we open fire
with the best weapons the 21st century can

offer to the men of the 19th." Mark smiled wide before hitting the pipe again. "Now we are here, no one knows why we were given this chance. And we agreed to fight. Well I say let's take the fight head-on, do what we do best and let God and history decide what to do with us! I, for one, do not want to run and hide from everyone in the country while I slowly die, doing nothing, afraid to see where this opportunity takes me."

Captain Pike stepped forward, "What say the Cubes?"

The roar was deafening as smiles overtook the Marines. Even Thompson shouted as he held the cold compress against the swelling on the back of his head from Brenners rifle butt.

"Wild Bill Sutton?" Mark shouted.

"Sir?" The sergeant stepped forward with a smile.

"Saddle the horses; we need to tell General Lee the Cubes want in this fight!" The roar renewed as the Sgt. grabbed two men and headed to the nearby horses.

Chapter Twelve

     The men rode to the Command tents
without the guide this time. It was just
past 10 p.m. according to Brian's pocket
watch. As they approached they watched the
smoke rising from the fires as the men
cooked their evening meals. The doctor's
tents were overflowing as before and men
were laid on the ground or in the backs of
wagons. The faint screams could be heard
even from this distance. Brian looked next
to the tent and saw the pile of amputated
limbs covered in flies as a soldier dumped
a bucket of fresh parts onto the pile.

     General Lee's staff had moved into a
cabin on the inside edge of the encampment.
Smoke and small sparks rose from the
chimney as a group of junior officers stood
off to the side smoking their pipes and
cigars. The horses, tied up to the posts,
were unusually calm as they drank and ate
from buckets set before them.

     Mark and Brian saluted the Captain as
he held the door open for them. As they
walked inside they were taken back by the
scene. General Lee stood behind a large
table with maps strewn on its top. The
history books flashed into both Marine

officers' minds as they instantly knew the gathered generals. Longstreet stood at Lee's right, his long black and grey beard making his name obvious. Around the table stood Generals A.P. Hill, and Ewell. With Jeb Stuart standing to the Commanders left. His Grandfather was there along with three other Colonels they didn't recognize.

"Gentleman, I am not getting good reports from today's battle. How is General Hood?"

"Sir," General Longstreet stepped forward. "He is not well sir. They gave him morphine for the pain and the surgeon was doing all he could but still unsure of his recovery." The gathered men looked down and said a quick prayer for their friend.

"So we gained a little ground on the flanks. And now with General Stuart's brigade here I think we can hit them hard and force the victory we were so close to today. Gentleman, in the morning we are going to hit the North right in the center." Lee's soft but commanding voice rose above the crackling fire as his hand swept across parts of the map. "I will have Jeb's brigade reinforce our left flank. General Longstreet," he looked to his right. "I want your division to go straight up the middle. We will start by pounding the enemy positions with cannon fire and drive them from their fortifications. Then your men will cross the field and finish driving them off the high ground. They are weak in the middle gentleman. I can feel it. I saw it this morning. They will break

if we hit them hard and fast." General Lee
stood back and looked to his officers for
replies.

"General," Longstreet was the only one
willing to speak. "General my men will have
to cross a half a mile of open ground to
achieve what you're asking. The Union
troops are hiding behind this low wall," He
traced his finger along with the map. "They
have perfect ground to fight from. We will
need buckets to catch the lead, sir."

"That is why we will hit them with
every cannon we can muster for a time
before sending the men forward, to drive
them off this low wall and make an attack
all the more possible," Lee spoke in a
matter-of-fact tone as he had already seen
his victory.

"Sir," General Longstreet pleaded for
over fifteen minutes for General Lee to
change his mind. The two marines stood a
few paces back and listened as the
arguments were made from both sides. Both
men were in awe as history was unfolding
around them.

"General Lee?" the voice from the
doorway interrupted.

"Yes, what is it?" the men looked to
the Captain.

"Sorry to interrupt you sir, but I am
told to inform you General Pickett and his
unit is arriving sir."

"Very well, thank you, Captain." He saluted the man as he shut the door.

"Excuse me, General Lee?" Mark spoke finally as he and Brian stood to attention.

"Oh, Major Peterson, I didn't realize you were here. You have something to add sir?"

Mark moved forward. "Sir, I have to agree in part with General Longstreet sir."

"In part?" Lee replied quizzically.

"Yes, sir. My men ambushed a small 100 man group trying to sneak through the bottom of Wolf's hill sir. A mix of cavalry and infantry on General Ewell's left flank. We sent maybe ten or eleven running but killed the rest. Now my scouts report…"

Brian cocked his head slightly, trying not to smile knowing they had not sent a single scout out. Mark was going by history. "Let's just hope history hasn't changed that much yet." Brian thought to himself as he continued to listen.

"…Report that General Meade is sending fresh troops to bolster his center and right flank. May I sir?" Mark motioned towards the maps.

"Of course Major," Lee replied.

Mark showed where history told him the Northern army would be, come morning. "Sir they sent a Corp of infantry here, right near Ewell's mid-section on the first curve of the fish hook. He has a brigade of Calvary to the southeast of his position in case of a flanking maneuver that direction. He has also pulled a division from his left flank and had a fresh division arrive and moved them both to the center of the hook, spreading them out along this line," His finger tracing the details again. "Right to where you plan on having General Longstreet attack sir."

"Major, how can you possibly know all this information? My scouts have not confirmed any of this yet?" General Lee asked with surprise.

"Sir, my men are the best. I have scouts that could watch you for three days, and report on what you ate and when you slept without you or your men knowing they were even there sir." Mark spoke with pride.

"Ok, son, you have an idea in your head, I can see it. Let's hear what you have to say." General Lee ordered as the other Generals looked on in disbelief at the audacity of this junior officer.

Mark took a deep breath before beginning. "Sir I suggest you move General Stuart as you ordered. He can reinforce General Ewell's right flank and right-center. Also form General Longstreet's men as planned and start the cannon barrage to the Union Center. This will make Meade think he guessed correctly about a frontal attack. After I think the North has decided

to concentrate on this potential attack, I
will move my men to the left flank of
General Ewell's group and begin our attack
from there. I will start with sharpshooters
from a thousand yards to put the fear into
the enemy."

"You cannot possibly hit them from
that far out with a rifle Major!" General
Hill said incredulously.

This time Captain Pike stepped
forward, "Sir, our men can hit them from
farther out than that if needs be."

"Let's leave that for a moment," Lee
interrupted. "Continue Major."

"We will also use our portable cannons
to drive them back. When ready I will send
my men forward under cover fire and destroy
the northern right flank. When we
accomplish this we can march into Meade's
command tents and finish the fight."

"Just like that," Stuart laughed out
loud as other Generals joined in.

"Yes general," Mark turned to look the
man in the eye. "Just like that." General
Stuart stopped laughing before Mark
continued. "You have no idea the amount of
firepower my unit has and will bring down
on the enemy." He looked back to General
Lee and Longstreet. "General, I promise you
this. My men will take the enemy by
surprise and decimate any we see. My
sharpshooters will engage them from a
distance where they have no idea who is

shooting them. They will fire cannons in our direction but we will be beyond their effective range. Our cannons, however, will engage groups of gathered men, supplies and officers and destroy them with extreme prejudice. When the timing is right we will charge their lines and destroy them."

A few of the gathered Generals felt a cold chill at the determination of Mark's voice. Stuart wanted to smile at the absurdity but decided to wait. He looked down to the Major's side and saw the handle of his pistol sticking out. It was not like any he had seen before. It appeared flat, with no cylinder to hold the rounds. And why were their uniforms a patchwork of different colors? These men had no idea how to be "Gentleman Officers." He thought to himself before returning to the maps.

"Gentlemen, would you mind stepping outside for a moment while I discuss this with my officers?" Lee asked the two Marines.

Both snapped to attention and saluted. "Yes, Sir!" They turned on their heels and headed out the door. When outside they moved off the porch and went to talk with Sgt. Bill Sutton and the other sergeant holding their steeds.

"Well Major?" Bill asked as he watched Mark light his pipe with a small wooden match.

"Nice speech, by the way, Mark," Brian spoke as he took a swig from his flask.

"You have been practicing that one or something?" The three men laughed quietly.

"We shall see I guess. I tried to make it sound as best I could. I would love to show them what we can do but why spoil the surprise." The men laughed as they turned to take in the sights of an actual confederate military camp. The sounds of a banjo joining in with a mouth harp and harmonica carried in the air. The fires began to burn low as the soldiers stopped tending them to get some rest from their busy day.

A sergeant walked by with a tray of hot cornbread. "Excuse me, sirs. We had a large shipment of supplies come in with the latest unit. So I made the men a surprise. Most won't get any till breakfast but I figured since the officers are still awake…" He let his voice trail off as the men all grabbed a large chunk, the tops still moist with butter.

"Thank you, Sergeant," The men all spoke before sampling the cook's skills. The smell hit them first before their stomachs took over and they bit into the soft delight they held. None of the Marines spoke as they savored each bite. A little more course than anything they had eaten before and not the bright yellow of the modern cornmeal but a lot more flavor.

"Damn," Brian said as he licked his fingers. "History sure does taste good." The men all laughed as they repeated Brian's gesture to their own fingers.

It was midnight before they were ordered back into the cabin. "Gentleman," General Lee spoke as the other generals looked on. While most of the officers gathered do not believe you can do what you say you can. Colonel Peterson here," He gestured to the man at the end of the table to his left. "He states he believes in you and your men, having seen some of your training last year in Georgia. That being said we will go with your plan of attack. If however, we do not hear of victory on your side of the battlefield by three o'clock, I will then order Longstreet's men to attack the center. We should have the cannons in place by eleven o'clock in the morning. When you hear them start to fire, I will give you one hour before I expect you to start your attack. General Ewell will have Major General Early keep his men off to your right flank so they can watch and report. They will also be ordered to attack when you make your breakthrough in the lines. Good luck and God be with you Gentleman!" General Lee saluted the pair to signal them to leave.

"Sir!" the men again snapped a salute before turning and heading outside.

"Well Major," Brian smiled, "Time to put up or shut up!" He laughed as he stepped into the stirrup and mounted his horse.

"Once more unto the breach dear friends," Mark replied with a smile and the three took off for their camp.

Chapter Thirteen

General Meade called his commanding officers to his tent. The generals updated the maps and spoke about the events of the day. General Meade stood back as the changes were made. Steam from his coffee rose and mingled with the cigar smoke in the air. "Gentleman, thank you. Now with Generals Sykes and Sedgwick in control of both Little and Big Round Tops, I am positive our left flank is secure. I have ordered the movement of two more batteries of artillery to the center of our lines. I want them to hold fire until the soldiers start their charge. I am sure the south with open up with a huge artillery barrage to drive us from the center. They have hit both our flanks and been turned back. General Lee has to think our middle is weak."

"Sir," General Sykes stepped forward. "I have relieved the 20th Maine and sent them to bolster the middle. They are tired from the battle on Little Round Top yesterday but we will give them food and ammunition when they arrive here and they say they will fill the reserve. I have sent a unit of sharpshooters from Michigan to assist."

"Very good. Now I have also sent the
newest arriving Corp to bolster our right
flank at Culp's Hill." Meade took a moment
to light his cigar and finish his coffee.
The other officers took turns studying the
map and discussing possible changes.
"Gentleman return to your units, get some
sleep, tomorrow will decide the outcome of
the battle and I fear the war." He let that
thought sink in for a moment before
finishing. "God be with you all. I will
send runners if there are any changes in
the morning."

The officers turned to leave, "General
Slocum, would you stay for a moment."

"Of Course General," The man stepped
to the side as the General staff exited the
tent. He turned and approached as Slocum
took a moment to sit in his chair and pull
from his cigar. "How can I be of service
sir?"

"Henry, I have sent several scouts out
and none have found any evidence of this
special unit from the South."

"Yes sir," The general replied looking
down to the floor.

"I am not saying your man was wrong,
Henry. I saw the look in his eyes and the
fear on his face. So I know he saw
something but what it could be I have no
idea." Meade took another mouthful of smoke
before continuing. "Henry I don't see the
point in telling the story and worrying the
men without proof."

"Of course not sir, let's just hope it was a mistake and we will not hear from them again." Meade offered the General a glass of whiskey and a chair. "Thank you, sir," the man spoke as he took a seat across from his General. "Honestly it sounded like a very small unit at best. Buchannan only saw about ten men. It sounded like a squad sent for the purpose of the ambush only." He pulled a pouch from within his coat and opened it. He packed the pipe with good southern tobacco and lit it with a match. He took a pull and let the smoke dance around his mouth before exhaling it towards the ceiling of the tent.

"I agree with Henry. At most it has to be a unit of what, maybe 40-50 men? How else could they have built special weapons without us hearing about it?" General Meade smiled back. He knew the North had spies everywhere. The men sat in silence for a few minutes, smoking and taking sips from their glasses. "Henry, do you think I am missing something?"

"General, I think your plans are excellent. You have made a lot of good decisions so far and your thinking makes perfect sense as to Lee's plans."

"Yes, your right. It's just pre-battle jitters I guess. Happens to the best of us right?" Meade smiled at his friend. When the pair had emptied their glasses he stood. "Henry," he stood and offered his hand. "Return to your men, get some sleep and god bless you tomorrow."

Slocum stood and shook the General's hand. "Thank you, sir, we shall drink our victory tomorrow." The general walked out of the tent and put his hat back on. He walked towards his horse stopping to look over the fires flickering in the growing darkness. The noise of moving men slowly died down as the Army of the Potomac tried to get some rest.

Chapter Fourteen

    Captain Brian Pike awoke early to
check on the sentries. He walked to find
the men awake and eager for the day's
events. Next he walked to the cook tent,
the smell of bacon and coffee drew him in.
He entered to find Corporal Engleman with
an apron on and directing two privates
around the kitchen. "Morning Men." He
watched as the men stopped and stood at
attention. "Sorry, at ease boys, as you
were."

    "Good morning Captain. Coffees fresh
and hot on the stovetop. Breakfast will be
served shortly."

    "It smells amazing Doug. Where did you
learn to cook?

    "My grandmother and my mother sir.
They told me if I learned to cook I would
impress the ladies." He smiled as he turned
the bacon in the large skillet in front of
him. The tent held three stoves, all wood-
fired with the smokestacks rising up
through holes in the roof of the tent.
Private Davis was cooking scrambled eggs by
the dozen while Private Erickson had two
Dutch ovens outside the side of the tent
baking fresh sourdough biscuits. A tray
held the first two batches on the table to

the right of the stoves. "Have a biscuit while you wait, sir," Doug pointed to the pile. "Butter right next to them sir. Whatever sent us here broke the rules as far as food was concerned," He laughed again. History says the South was not well supplied.

Brian slathered some butter on the biscuit he ripped open and watched as it slowly melted into the cracks and crevasses of the dough. He took a half and shoved the whole thing in his mouth. His eyes closed as the tasty food was chewed and swallowed. "These are amazing Doug! Mother's recipe I am guessing?" He spoke quickly before taking a more modest bite from the remaining half.

"Yes, sir. She would have starter in the fridge all the time and every three days or so, she would make a batch of bread and biscuits. She taught me a cheat to make sourdough starter overnight and that's how we have this today." He spoke proudly of his mother's skills at teaching. "She taught me the better side of breakfast while grandma taught me dinner. Biscuits and gravy, breakfast casserole, roast, ribs, even desserts all made in cast iron, first over the fire or with hot coals. Grandma survived the depression as well as world war two. She taught me a lot about stretching ingredients and improvising in the kitchen. Mom was all about flavor and making sure no one left her table hungry. To be honest I almost didn't join the Marines and went to cooking school." He paused for a moment at the thought of where

100

he would be now if he had chosen the latter. "Well if we make it home I still have that option I guess." He laughed briefly as he lifted the lid off a cast iron pot on the table and forked in the cooked bacon. He grabbed a plate and put four slices on it, followed by a large spoonful of freshly cooked eggs and another biscuit before handing it to his Captain. "Bon appetite sir," He smiled handing the tin plate over.

"Thank you, Corporal," Brian replied as he moved to a table and sat on the bench seat. Brian got the first bite of eggs in his mouth as a dozen soldiers walked into the tent, rubbing their eyes free from the sleep in them.

The sounds of hungry soldiers filled the tent as they made up plates of food and moved outside to the fresh air. Doug and his helpers worked tirelessly to keep the food dishes full. Brian was so preoccupied with his food he missed Major Peterson and Lieutenant Brown when they came into the tent. He jumped when Mark set his plate down.

"Sorry, Brian didn't mean to startle you," Mark spoke as he sat on the bench across the table.

"Wow Sorry sir, I guess I let my mind drift a bit there. Morning Jerry," He nodded at the Lieutenant as he sat next to Mark. "The men seem to be waking up."

"Yes Sir," Jerry replied. "Of course with the smells emanating from this place they can't possibly sleep any longer." He laughed along with the two officers as he tested Engleman's brew. The three ate in silence for a few moments, enjoying the food. "I checked on the sentries at two and at four, they reported no movement," Jerry finally breaking the silence.

"I just checked on them again before stepping in here," Brian said after swallowing his mouthful of breakfast. "I figured we make sure the men are all awake by 0800 and have our first briefing at 0900. I was planning a weapon check at 0930 and head out by 1000 sir."

"Agreed Brian," Mark replied swallowing his own grub first. "Let's finish eating, make sure all the men have a full belly and then get this show on the road."

2nd lieutenant Phil Masters and Master Gunnery Sergeant Evans joined the table with plates of their own. The men discussed anything but the upcoming battle while they ate. The rest of the men came and went, preferring to eat outside. They sat on crates or logs near their tents or by the fires. The sun was rising above the trees finally as the men finished their meals. The walked the plates back to the cook tent and began prepping their weapons and packs for the fight.

Mark looked at his pocket watch as the hands reached 0900. "Jerry, assemble the men."

"Yes sir," Jerry saluted and turned. "Marines!" his voice boomed across the small camp. "Assemble for briefing!" the men stood from their makeshift seats and made their way quickly to the command tent.

"Men, today we get into the fight." Mark smiled at the gathered. We will move out at 1000 and make our way to the far right of the Confederate lines. We will position ourselves about a thousand yards from the enemy lines. The main unit will start the cannon fire on the center of Meade's lines, opposite us. When we think the Union has taken the bait, we will open fire with mortars and snipers and slowly demoralize the enemy." He paused as the six snipers and three mortar teams stood a little straighter and let smiles creep across their faces. "Captain Pike?"

"We will keep this up for about an hour or so. If the enemy remains in their positions we will move the rest of the Cubes up and attack directly." Brian let the broad strokes sink in before continuing. "Men, it is a big open area we have to cross but we will have the cover of the snipers and mortars. Unlike Pickett's charge, I know the snipers alone will scare the hell out of those Northern boys. The .50's can take out two men at a time if they give us the chance. Mortar teams will concentrate on groups, cannons and supply stores."

Mark took the reins again. "First and second fire teams with Recon team 1 will form on the left with snipers and mortars in the middle and third and fourth interdiction teams with recon team 2 on the right. We will keep everything else fluid and make plans as they develop."

"Weapons check at 0930, we move out at 1000 hrs," Brian spoke loudly. "This is not our first fight men but we can honestly say what we do today will change history. Dismissed!"

Chapter Fifteen

The day was growing hot in the early
July sun as the Marines waited for the
kickoff. They had set up in a line inside
the tree line, 30 feet back from the edge.
Lieutenant Jerry Brown watched through his
binoculars as men and horse moved about the
enemy lines. The fight was close; he could
feel it in his bones.

He looked at his men briefly, their
jaws set, rifles ready, and fingers off the
triggers. He was in charge of the fire
group. He had members from Fireteam One and
Two from Interdiction and Recon team one.
His squad would cover the southern or
leftmost flank of the unit. Jerry placed a
three-man unit facing south in case the
Northern Calvary unit in the area decided
to come and play. Knowing his men were in
position he moved along the line, in the
trees towards the center. Passing through
his men he found Major Peterson and Captain
Pike.

"Your men all set Lieutenant?" Mark
asked as Jerry approached.

"Yes, sir. The men are ready and
willing sir," Jerry replied as he watched
the snipers ready their positions. Sergeant
Alex Natole had his .50 set on a fallen

tree. Alex had made a nice snipers perch using a large log to sit on. "Nice setup Sergeant."

"It's quite a comfortable spot, sir." He smiled as he looked through the scope. He was deep enough in the tree line that it would be difficult for the enemy to see him. "I have a good arch of fire and nice cover in case some lucky schmuck gets close."

"Sergeant," Captain Pike asked," Range?"

"I show 997 yards to the outside edges of their line and 950 to the center sir."

"Very well," Brian answered as he looked to the others. They had Master Gunnery Sergeant Tyler Evans on the left side of the group next to Sergeant Gary Yarger, both had their suppressed .308 caliber rifles set. They had found good, dry flat ground. They pulled some downed branches and brush to make a bit of cover and concealment to their front. Sergeant Brenner had the second .50 and was on Natole's right. The remaining two snipers set up on Brenner's right. Each of the sharpshooters was ten yards apart. Everyone looked to the west as the cannon barrage started on the opposite side of the battlefield.

"Alright boys, the curtain just went up. We have about an hour." The men settled down in their spots and seemed to relax for a moment. "Smoke 'em if you got 'em." Mark

bellowed as he pulled his own pipe and bag
of tobacco from his inside jacket pocket.
He noticed he had been smoking more since
he arrived, but the tobacco was really
good. "Brian, Jerry?" He said through his
teeth that held the pipe in his mouth as he
lit it with the match.

"Sir?" the two men said in unison.
Both men had a cigar in his mouth.

"Well, what did I miss?" Mark asked in
all seriousness.

"Nothing sir," Brian replied first.
The men are set up in good firing
positions. The long-range will confuse the
hell out of the enemy, especially since
they won't…" Brian's voice trailed off as
he looked to the enemy positions.

"Captain?" Mark asked realizing the
man had stopped mid-sentence.

"Brian?" Jerry asked as he nudged the
man with his elbow.

"Oh sorry sir, but what if? What if we
let the suppressed rifles start taking the
occasional shot now?" He looked down to
find Evans smiling. "They can't see us from
this distance. They won't hear the shots.
All they will know is some of the men just
start dying. As the hour mark approaches we
slowly increase their rate of fire. Then
when the clock strikes we open up with the
.50's and then the mortars. When the .50's
shoot they will see men dying and two
seconds later hear the report of the

rifles. After a couple of minutes of that, we start the mortars. They will already be confused but then shit will start to blow up without a sound of cannon fire. If that doesn't scare the hell out of them, nothing will." Brian smiled at the possibilities of the plan.

Jerry took a long pull on his cigar, his smile widens as he released the smoke. "I like it, sir, I like it a lot."

"I have to agree with you both. That's a damn fine plan Captain. He looked to Sergeant Evans, "You two fire one round each and make sure it kills someone. Lieutenant Brown, go tell the other two .308's to do the same. Have them take a shot every ten minutes. At 1130 hours shorten that to one shot every five. At 1200 hours we will release the rest in tandem."

"Copy that sir," Jerry almost giggled back as he made his way through the trees and brush to the remaining snipers.

Sergeants Evans and Yarger pulled their weapons tight into their shoulders. "I have an officer on horseback just left of the tree," Evans announced to his shooting partner.

"Copy that, I will take the sergeant standing at the line behind his men," Yarger replied.

Evans slowly pulled on the trigger until it snapped. Mark stood behind him

with his binoculars pointed at the officer
target. He increased the magnification
until only the officer and the tree were in
his view. Yarger shot 2 seconds later. Both
men were visible to the other two officers
watching through their binoculars. Mark
noticed the Officer was a Colonel as the
man was struck in the chest. He watched as
the breath was knocked from him, he
staggered for a moment before falling from
the saddle.

Jerry and Brian watched as the back of
the Sergeant's head exploded on contact
from the .308. The man fell like a log. All
the men nearby looked at the fallen men
with stunned disbelief. The horse never
moved at being relieved at the loss of
weight from its back. Jerry swung his
binoculars to the right as the remaining
two snipers let their bullets fly. Two men,
a private and a lieutenant both died
silently as their fellow soldiers looked
surprised.

All four racked a new round into the
chamber and Mark watched as the empty
casings disappeared midair. "Well that will
start them thinking," he smiled as he
watched a few men shout orders along the
enemy lines. "Let them think on that for a
few before reminding them," Mark ordered
with a smile. "Jerry return to your squad,
rest for a bit. We will all be busy soon
enough."

"Roger that sir. Happy hunting boys,"
Jerry said as he walked back south along
the line.

2nd Lieutenant Phil Masters had his men set up on the right flank of their group. He knew the plan and watched as the snipers fired early. He figured if he needed to know they would send a runner. He watched the enemy through his binoculars until he heard horses approaching. He looked to see an officer and 2 sergeants on horseback ride through the trees towards him.

"Lieutenant?" the man spoke as he pulled the reins on his mount. "Lieutenant Davison sir. General Ewell wished me to inform you we are on your right. We will support any breakthrough you make." The Confederate officer looked to the man and was confused by his uniform. The pack looked like nothing his men had, nor had he ever seen. The patchwork of colors on the shirt and pants looked like it was made by mistake. The rifle confused him most. Officers didn't carry rifles, just pistols, and swords. This man had a pistol but no sword. The rifle had no ramrod, nor a hammer for the percussion cap. How in God's name did he fire the thing? He wondered.

"2nd Lieutenant Masters sir, I have runners ready if we need you." He returned the salute and watched as all three horsemen slowly turned their steeds around, not able to look away till they started back north to their units. Phil looked at one of his men sitting against a tree that watched the event. "I think they are totally confused Corporal." Phil smiled at the man.

"I believe your right sir. I wish I could hear what they tell their men when they get back."

"Y'all ain't gonna believe the rifles they be carrying," Masters spoke in a bad thick southern accent. "Not sure where they load it, or how the hell they be firing it." The two men had a laugh before Phil turned and began looking at the enemy again.

Ten minutes passed slowly before the snipers took their next shot. This time they all aimed at officers on horseback. Brian heard Evans call his target and found him with his binoculars. This was a Captain sitting high on his horse just in front of a group of three junior officers. He was very animated in whatever he was telling them, his arms flailing left and right to spots up and down the line. Sergeant Evans pulled the trigger as the man turned his head to the side. The faces of the junior officers turned bright red as they were splashed with the contents of the Captain's head being ejected out of the exit wound. The captain fell in a heap at the feet of their horses.

Sgt. Yarger counted to five after Evans shot before sending his own bullet downrange. He hit the lieutenant behind the captain as the man tried to wipe the blood from his face. His bullet went through the man's hand before entering the officer's cheek and exiting the backside of his head. He pulled hard on the reins as he fell, startled the horse and sent it running.

Mark watched as the other two officers scattered, one riding hard towards the back of the pack and the other shouting orders as he poured a canteen over his face riding down the line towards Mark's left flank.

A unit of cannon were moved forward and began firing from the Union lines. The first two volleys fell short of the trees. "MORTARS," Peterson yelled, silence those things before they get range.

The two mortar teams were twenty yards back from the snipers. The sergeants in charge of each team ranged the target and gave coordinates. "Hang," the sergeants yelled as a corporal held the end of the mortar round in the tube. "Fire," the sergeant commanded and the corporal released the round to fall down the tube. The team all leaned away from the tube as the round was fired behind a pressure wave. Their rounds fell dead center of each group as the enemy cannons exploded sending shrapnel into the men nearby. 12 out of fifteen enemy soldiers died instantly. The enemy was confused since they heard no cannon return fire before their weapons exploded.

The sergeants sighted in the next cannon and the process was repeated with the same results. Five rounds were sent from each mortar and within 3 minutes, ten Union cannons were destroyed along with close to a hundred soldiers. Mark looked to see some of the cannon soldiers beginning to move away from their posts. "Send another round each," Mark ordered. He felt

the pressure wave wash over him as both
teams sent another round simultaneously.
Two cannons explode next to each other. A
piece of hot shrapnel must have hit the
powder stores as a third explosion occurred
behind the left cannon and sent men and
horse flying. "Yeah!" a few of the Marines
shouted as the extra explosion hit.

"Hold Fire," Mark ordered as he waited
to see how the enemy reacted. He noticed no
enemy soldier was standing next to any
remaining cannon. "Let's see how they
respond to that Captain. Then we will
really pour it on." Mark smiled at Brian as
they looked away from the enemy for a
moment.

Chapter Sixteen

General Meade stood outside his command tent using his binoculars to see the battlefield to his west. The sounds of cannon fire from the Confederates were almost continuous. He pulled the binoculars away from his eyes as riders approached.

"Sir," the lieutenant saluted as he stopped his horse. "They report an extremely large gathering of cannon on the ridge side at our center. At least one hundred and fifty plus cannon and they are hitting us hard there."

"Very well," Meade replied, "Have the men hold their position and prepare for an enemy charge. Tell our artillery to not fire yet, save their shots for when the infantry advance."

"Yes sir," the officer replied and saluted as he pulled the reins to the right and kicked the horse into a gallop.

"Sir, the next man said as he stopped his horse.

"Yes Sergeant," Meade replied without the salute.

"General Sykes and Sedgwick report
they are taking fire but no charge yet.
They are holding strong with minimal
casualties."

"Very good sergeant," Meade replied as
he moved into the command tent and started
moving pieces on the map.

"150 cannons? My God, I have never
heard of such a gathering of guns." One of
the gathered officers sputtered as the
sound of cannon fire gave proof to the
statement.

"You were right sir. Lee is
concentrating on our middle. That many guns
mean he is trying to soften us up for his
infantry." Another spoke proudly.

"I agree gentleman, it seems Lee means
to take our middle. He is not doing much on
the flanks yet." General Meade spoke
strongly and with a bit of hope.

"General Meade sir?" The men turned to
see two lieutenants at the edge of the
tent. "General Howard reports a smattering
of cannon fire and infantry to the
northwest but no major attack." The first
one spoke before being dismissed and
turning around to walk away.

"Yes," General Meade spoke to the air,
his eyes glued to the map.

"Sir, General Slocum sir, he is not
sure how to report this," the man stuttered
in his speech.

"Report what Lieutenant?"

"Sir, we have been taking fire of some sort from the extreme right flank. We have had several officers just shot off their horses but no rifle report to go with it. General Slocum ordered the cannons to fire on the tree line where he is sure the Grey backs are hiding sir. The first couple of volleys fell short. They were adjusting their range when we lost twelve cannons in maybe five minutes, no sound of cannon fire being directed on them. Somehow their shots were perfect, not near-misses sir but direct hits. Over two hundred men dead in minutes," the lieutenant exaggerated a bit but it had to be close from what he saw.

The gathered command staff stood silent at the report. "Lieutenant, show me where on the map," Meade ordered. The lieutenant moved forward and pointed to the trees on the map where the shots were believed to come from.

"How can cannon just explode without being hit by other cannons?" How can cannon fire not be heard that's only, what? A thousand yards maybe more. Our cannons fire farther than that with ease?" Who can shoot that far with a rifle and hit a target let alone kill him?" The gathered officer's questions came on top of each other.

"Lieutenant, ride to General Howard and see if he can spare any cannon to send to Slocum's aide. Have him move a unit of reserves to bolster Slocum's line. Have them hold fast and prepare for an infantry attack. Dismissed." Meade turned to his officers. "Gentlemen, I still believe the major point of attack will be from our west in our center. Lee has too many cannons to be just a diversion. We will stick to our original plans. Bolster the center, conserve our artillery till we see the infantry and destroy them on the open ground as they march towards us." Meade spoke with the confidence of a commanding general who knew he would win the fight.

Chapter Seventeen

Major Peterson checked his pocket watch, three minutes to the hour mark. He walked over to his mortar teams, "How are we set for ammo Sergeant?"

The man turned and lifted the wooden lid off the top ammo box. In the thirty minutes since they had last fired and destroyed the cannons, the ammo box had been refilled. "Full load of twenty rounds per box sir," He said with a smile. "I don't know what is doing this but I like it, sir." He laughed as the rest of his team smiled.

"Ok, do you have your targets picked sergeants?" He asked looking to both team leaders.

"Yes, sir. We have picked the first fifty targets, the obvious ones of course, and divided them between the three teams so we don't waste ammo." Sergeant Maleski of mortar team two replied.

"Excellent, only a minute or so now boys. Let's get ready to scare the hell out of the blue bellies." He smiled as he turned and walked forward towards the .50 caliber snipers perches. Looking through his binoculars he could see the enemy cannons stood empty. Not one soldier wanted to get anywhere near them. So far Captain

Pike's plan seems to be working. "Sergeant Evans, you ready to begin?" He asked without looking away from the enemy as he watched as a few men moved laterally along the low rock wall.

"Sir, they have stacked up nicely. To be honest," he looked away from his scope for a moment as Mark turned to meet his eyes. "At this distance, I should be able to end two or three at a time. This rifle they will hear, but only two or three seconds after the man next to them has died." A wicked grin grew across his face as he settled back and pulled the butt of his rifle to his shoulder.

"Well then, Sergeant, you may start the music whenever you please," Mark smiled back as he took a knee and prepared for the pressure wave of the .50, followed by the mortar teams.

Tyler decided to make the first round extra special. He focused on three men at the front of the wall, two privates and a sergeant. The private in front had his rifle laying on the top of the wall as the man behind him was turned and speaking to the sergeant. He slowly pulled on the trigger till it snapped, it felt like a small glass tube breaking behind his fingertip. The force on his shoulder was a surprise to the man, just like he had been trained. His rifle settled down and he found his sight as the bullet hit the man in front. The shower of blood and tissue expanded as the .50 caliber bullet passed through all three men, throwing one into

the other. The massive mist of blood hit a
horse in the face standing four feet behind
the men and startled it. The beast bucked
hard and threw its rider, a lieutenant, off
its back and down to the ground, breaking
his arm. Three seconds later the men to the
right and left heard the massive crack of
the big gun. The private just to the left
began shaking violently and wet his pants
at the sight of the three men. The
sergeants left arm dangled by a small piece
of skin and fabric. Another soldier vomited
over the wall after looking at the carnage,
his breakfast slowly dripping down the
rocks and mortar.

Fifty yards to their left another
three men were thrown backward as Sergeant
Natole's bullet ripped through them. He had
fired at a slight upwards angle due to the
hill the wall skirted, His bullet went into
the chest of the first, exited and entered
high in the chest of the next before
ripping through the throat of the third
causing the head to fly further backward
before hitting the green grass and rolling
back to meet the shoulders of its former
owner. The mix of blood turned the grass
red and the dirt almost black. Soldiers
looked to their fallen comrades as the two
mortars sent a round each downrange.

With no warning, two supply wagons
exploded in a massive fireball sending the
drivers and the horses meant to pull them
flying. Musket balls were sent in all
directions as men nearby took hits. The
screams from the wounded filled the air.
Men at the wall began to duck as four more

were taken out, the sounds of the two rifles filling their ears seconds after they died.

"All snipers, open fire! Mortars weapons free!" Mark shouted as the men began doing what they were best at. Staff Sergeant Roger Klomp led the first mortar team. He quickly gave new target info and they sent a single round into a group of four officers on horseback. Man and beast turned to a grizzly mass of blood and tissue as they were blown apart. He followed with another round into a supply wagon before seeing a group of men running for the cannons. He waited a moment before sending a round at them.

Sergeant Tim Goodman was the leader of the second mortar team. He destroyed three wagons in less than 90 seconds. His men were shifting targets as fast as he called them out. He was calling his next target as something caught his eye from the right. He shifted his binoculars to find a new unit of artillery arriving, the horses were slowing down and turning to allow the cannons to be unhooked and readied to shoot. "Ok boys," he gave the starting coordinates, "five quick rounds, sweeping left ten yards at a time." He ordered as the men made the quick adjustments. "Fire!" He said a bit loud but he was excited.

The rounds landed dead on the first cannon, sending its parts in all directions. The horse took off at a dead run, piece of wood shrapnel sticking out of its backside. The two men driving the cannon were thrown off by the blast. Both men were gravely wounded from the explosion. The mortar team swept down the line and destroyed three of the five targets with direct hits. The other two were close enough to blast the cannons from their wheels. "Well done men," he shouted. Men and beast ran in all directions, the men tried to find cover where ever they could.

"Let's see what to blow up next." He said out loud. He had a brief moment of doubt, thinking this was too easy. It lasted only a moment until he began to hear the enemy soldiers firing their rifles at them. He knew they couldn't even dream of reaching them but he also knew the Union had over ten thousand men on this patch of the battlefield alone. Given what they were doing he figured they would kill him if they could. So he shook off the unwanted feeling and shouted "Next target." An infantry unit was marching into his area in formation; forty men were killed or wounded in the blast. When both teams had fired their first twenty rounds they moved the empty box to the side and placed the wooden cover on tight. They all hoped whatever was orchestrating this would refill the boxes when they lifted the cover again.

Chapter Eighteen

"General Slocum, the men are taking massive fire but…" the Captain stood in front of his General stiff as a board.

"But what," General Slocum asked as he turned from the maps on the table in front of him. "My God Captain, you're as white as a sheet."

"Sir, it's just. Well, we have no sound of cannon firing and only the report of one or two rifles but men are literally being blown in half and the cannons and supply wagons just explode." The Captain looked like he would pass out. Beads of sweat poured from his forehead as he spoke. "We lost all five cannons that were diverted here by General Meade's order. They didn't have a chance to even unhook them from the horses. General Howard sent two regiments from XI Corp to bolster our lines. They arrived in formation and within seconds lost a third of the men. The German regiment took the most loses." He spoke rapidly before the General held up a hand.

"Take a moment Captain," He told the junior officer as one of the colonels held out a canteen for the man. The general stepped to his desk and grabbed his flask, pouring two fingers worth into a tin cup for the man. "Here this will calm you down." The general handed the man the cup as concern grew on his face.

"Thank you, sir," the man finally spoke after taking a swig of the whiskey. The captain took a second drink and the gather command staff watched his shoulders finally drop an inch or two as he relaxed.

"Continue your report Captain," the general ordered.

"Sir, Colonel Travis had the German unit stay on the left flank of your troops while he marched the other regiment to the middle where we have taken the most casualties. The men are scared, sir. No infantry has been spotted and we are unable to tell what exactly they are shooting at us with. We know the fire is coming from the trees but the only weapons that can reach them are the cannons."

"Why are they not firing Captain?" A colonel beat the other officers to the question.

"Sir, the men refuse to man the cannons. Anytime a unit approaches and begins to ready the cannon, they are killed, sir. The gun just explodes. We have fourteen working cannons left but no one willing to man them." The Captain paused for a moment as the news shook the officers. "The men are all hunkered down behind the wall and whatever large trees are left. They fired blindly for a few minutes before we got them to stop. Now

they are just scared, sir. The Colonel
requests instructions, sir?" The captain
finished the drink and handed the cup to a
Major who extended his hand to take it.

"General Geary," Slocum turned to his
Brigadier General in charge of a division
of his XII Corp. "What is the best equipped
and manned regiment?"

"Sir, I have the 7th Ohio Volunteers
with 400 men, as well as the 3rd Wisconsin
regiment with 375 men. They have both had a
full day of rest and each man carries
seventy-five rounds. They are ready for a
fight." The general stood proud at the
notification.

"Move them to the right flank. Have
one unit head towards the trees and draw
the enemy out of their perch. When the men
are halfway across the field, start the
second regiment to support. We will make
these unknown soldiers show their cards."

The captain turned on his heels and
headed back to his horse. "Colonel Stevens,
make haste to General Meade and inform him
of the situation as well as my plan to draw
the enemy out."

"Yes Sir," the colonel snapped as he
grabbed his sword and gloves from the table
near the door and headed outside.

"Can we see this flank from here?"
Slocum asked.

"Yes sir, we should be able to stay safe and still have a good view of the battle with our binoculars," a Major responded.

"Very well gentleman. Let's see what happens when we draw these grey backs out of hiding," the general spoke as he exited the cabin to the sounds of rifles and cannons from all directions.

Chapter Nineteen

Lieutenant Brown looked across the battlefield. He watched as two regiments of Union troops formed up and stood in unison. The first began marching towards them, rifles on their shoulders.

"First squad," he yelled. "Heads up! Looks like some boys wanna come to play." The men all moved from the seated position they had been relaxing in, to one knee. Every Marine looked at the sight of 400 soldiers heading their way. Some unconsciously checked their pouches for their spare magazines and grenades. A few had been practicing reloading their weapons with their magazines in the new holders.

Major Peterson had not stopped scanning the battlefield and quickly saw the marching troops. "Brian looks like first squad will be in contact soon.

Brian swung his binoculars to the left, "Yup, looks like 2 regiments, maybe 400 soldiers apiece." Brian studied the enemy for a moment. "Orders?"

"None yet. Let's keep the heavy fire on the bulk of the enemy. Send a runner to

2nd Squad and prepare them in case 1st needs help."

"Roger that," Brian replied as he pointed to a private. The man received his orders and took off at a run towards 2nd squad. "I have to admit I miss our radios, Major." Brian smiled as he watched the private reach 2nd squad.

"Me too Brian, Me too." Mark smiled behind his binoculars.

Jerry guessed the enemy was 600 yards away. "Sergeant Schanz, you ready with the SAW?"

"Yes, sir!" Sergeant John Schanz announced. Schanz was the bear of the Platoon. Six foot five and three hundred pounds with hands like meat hooks; he was tasked with carrying the M-249 Squad Automatic Weapon. It was called a light machine gun even though it weighed in at 22 pounds when fully loaded. John had its bipod open and resting on a felled tree trunk. He made a quick check to his left to make sure his next two boxes of ammo were close by. "Don't forget to close the boxes when empty," he said to himself as he pulled the charging handle to put the weapon in battery.

As soon as the marines heard this they all pulled on their charging handles, placing their thumbs on the safeties. "Make the shots count boys," Jerry ordered. "Don't forget their rifles are in range now so watch your ass." Jerry smiled as he let

the binoculars fall and grabbed his own
rifle. His breathing slowed as the wall of
blue approached closer. When he figured
they were under 500 yards he gave the
order. "Weapons free, open fire!" He
yelled.

The 3rd Wisconsin Regiment was a proud
group. They marched without showing fear,
knowing they were being used to bring the
enemy out into the open. They just wanted
to fight. They had heard the other men
talking about this hidden enemy that was
killing soldiers from afar and without
warning. They all saw the movement of a few
soldiers as they grew slightly from the
grass and from behind the trees. Each of
the soldiers brought their rifles off their
shoulders and began to march with them in
the ready position.

Their Colonel was on the far right
side of their lines when the tree line
opened up with a barrage of gunfire. They
had formed up in 4 lines of one hundred men
each. 40 of their fellow soldiers were
killed or injured in the first few seconds.
"Halt!" The Colonel order. "Make ready!" He
yelled as the remaining soldiers in front
dropped to a knee and the second row
brought their rifles up between the heads
of them. "Fire!" he bellowed as a cloud of
smoke obstructed their view for a moment.
The union soldiers began the process of
reloading, not knowing if they hit anyone.

The third and fourth rows moved to the
left and right of the first, stretching out
the line as they also prepared to fire. One

Private saw a head moving from the left side to the right side of a tree. He took aim and fired, trying to plan the man's next appearance. His mini-ball flew true and struck Sergeant Anderson in the throat. It tore through and splashed the tree behind him with blood and bone. The body swayed for a moment before falling backward, landing with a thud.

Schanz opened up with his SAW and took his time walking his fire across the front lines of the enemy. He would hold the trigger down in ten-round bursts, or as close as he could to ten rounds. He didn't want the barrel to overheat. Two bullets hit the tree in front of him and peppered him with shrapnel. Three pieces found their way into the exposed skin on the left side of his face. He saw three soldiers lifting their rifles and starting to reload. Assuming they were the ones that shot at him he altered his aim. "Son of a…" He pulled the trigger and killed the three, two still holding the paper cartridge in their teeth.

When his belt had run out he ducked behind the large tree and pulled a new belt out of the metal box he had opened. He layered the bullets in the box hooked to the side of the saw and made sure to close the lid tight on the now-empty ammo container. He pulled the charging handle twice to make sure a live round was seated in the chamber and sat up, letting the bipod find a new home on the trunk. He continued to fire in short bursts, watching as the enemy fell in front of him.

Colonel Davis of the 3rd Wisconsin took two steps back as he watched the tree line explode with fire. "They must have over a thousand men to be firing that fast!" He yelled out loud to no one. He turned and waved for the 7th Ohio to advance. A quick look down the line showed over half his men dead or wounded. "Forward!" He ordered as the bugler sounded the call. The men all stood and began marching forward, hoping to gain safety by overrunning the enemy position. The man playing the bugle was silenced as a bullet tore the bugle out of his hand. He looked to see the bent instrument a few feet away. When he turned back to the fight a round caught him the head. He stood for only a moment, blood running down his face from the hole left by the 21st-century weapon.

A recon team arrived and bolstered Jerry's position as the 7th Ohio regiment met up with the men from Wisconsin. Jerry made a quick look at his men as he dropped an empty magazine and reached for another. He had lost three men so far. His face showed relief as Sergeant Jon Pickleman showed up with the Recon team.

"Damn good timing Jon!" he shouted over the gunfire with a smile before turning and opening up on the now much closer enemy.

A mile to the east of the battle stood the men of the Third Cavalry Division, commanded by Brigadier General George Custer. They couldn't help but hear the massive artillery fire to the west. The men were dismounted and Custer stood with his junior officers in a small grove of trees. They were enjoying the shade and the small respite it gave them from the day's heat. The officers all stopped as two scouts approached.

"Report," Custer said deadpan as the men pulled their horses to a stop.

"Sir, We have heavy gunfire from the trees on the southeast part of the battlefield. We have no idea how many soldiers are in the tree line but we watched as they cut down most of the 3rd Wisconsin Volunteers. The 7th Ohio is coming up behind them but I worry they will face the same."

"What do you mean you don't know how many?" A Major spoke out of turn.

"Major, we did not see one soldier. With the rate of fire, there should be a thousand men but we can't see them. We did not want to get to close in case they spotted us but sir I saw one soldier and only one soldier. Not sure what he was carrying but he was firing 10 to 20 rounds for every volley of ours." The man's face was pale from both fear and dripping with sweat from the hard ride they made to report the news.

All the officers looked to the newest commander of their unit. Sergeant," he looked to the second man on horseback. "Ride and meet with General Gregg. Let him

know I am moving my unit to the west to
assist in the fight on our right flank."

"Yes sir!" the man replied as he
pulled the reins hard to the right and
kicked his horse into gear.

"Mount up the division we ride west,"
Custer ordered as he moved to his horse.

Chapter Twenty

General Meade stood stiff, his mouth
hanging open. He watched the battle from
outside his command post and could not
believe his eyes. His soldiers were falling
like wheat to the unseen enemy. He could
see small bursts of flames. What he could
not see was the cloud of smoke that comes
along with the muzzleloader or cannons
firing.

The soldiers had stopped advancing and
were furiously firing into the trees. He
watched as his Colonel moved down the line,
obviously shouting encouragement to the
men. Finally, he caught a glimpse of the
enemy as he saw shapes running to the right
from within the trees.

"We need to get reinforcements over
there, NOW!" he shouted. "Who can we send?"
He turned to look at his gathered officers.

"Sir, we have reports of enemy
engagements all along our line. The only
place where we are not in direct contact is
our left. We are taking heavy artillery
fire on that side." His number two spoke up
quickly. "We cannot pull from the left
because that is where Lee seems to be
concentrating in that direction. Scouts

report at least three Corps in the tree line."

"I agree but get me something or they will decimate our lines to the east!" Meade snapped back as he continued to watch the slaughter. "Send riders to each General. Send one unit from each reserve with all speed to bolster our right flank. Double time it Major!"

The major ran around the cabin shouting for runners. Meade and his officers watched as men from the wall were being brought back to the medical tents. Most were dead. The few injured were writhing in pain and shouting about not hearing the gunshot that hit them. A few mentioned how they were hit after the bullet passed through two or three men first. "What can do this?" Meade asked himself before looking along the wall with bare eyes. His men were all hunkered down below the wall. Some were lying flat, clutching their rifles hard to their chests. No one made a move in fear of being targeted.

The M-60 crew from Interdiction team two set up ten feet to Schanz's right. The large trunk was the perfect height for the gunner and loader to kneel behind it and have a good field of fire. Schanz felt the tree move as the gunner dropped the twenty-three-pound weapon down. Sergeant Brian Fisher opened fire with the 7.62mm weapon and the bark was heard by all. He sent two and three-second bursts across the open field and mowed down the soldiers as they

knelt to take aimed shots. They had made it
to within two hundred yards of the marines
but it had cost them a full regiment. The
two gunners killed twenty men in seconds.

Several men of the 7th Ohio regiment
had dropped their weapons and were running
hard south. The remaining soldiers were
firing as fast as they could. The officers
were shouting encouragement as they moved
up and down the line. Captain Stevens had
taken a round to the shoulder. He packed
the wound with a bandage and got back up.
He was unable to move his right arm. He
picked up his sword with his left hand and
continued to move among his men. Seeing his
bravery twenty men stood rapidly and
charged the enemy, screaming like madmen as
they ran.

Jerry Brown had just slammed a fresh
magazine into his weapon when he heard the
screams and saw the men running at him. He
stood and moved out from his cover in the
trees. Raising his rifle, he emptied the 30
round magazine into the charging men,
killing 12 and seriously wounding the rest.
He fell back as an enemy bullet tore
through his upper left leg. "Medic!" He
screamed as he dragged himself back around
the tree. He slammed his right hand onto
the wound as he grabbed for his tourniquet.

In the future, the officer would have
had a tourniquet made of polymer with a
built-in rod to increase the pressure and
Velcro straps to hold the rod tight. He
reached into his pack and pulled a thick,
wide strap out. He tied it above the wound

on his thigh and looked around the ground
near him. He found a stick he knew was
thick enough to handle the pressure, so he
wrapped the ends of leather around it tying
a tight knot. He spun the stick hard making
him winch in pain as the bleeding stopped.

"What happened LT?" Petty Officer
Michael Brown asked as he knelt next to the
officer.

"Lucky shot, Doc. Damn this hurts."
Jerry spoke as he gritted his teeth.

The medic pulled his knife and cut
away at the wool pants. He reached around
the thigh and his hand came back with blood
on it. "Ok sir, good news. It passed
straight through and it missed your femur."
He smiled as he pulled a cotton bandage and
a glass jar from his pack. "Better news is
we still have clotting powder," he smiled
as he pulled the stopper from the jar. "Bad
news is whatever sent us back decided to
take it out of the bandages and gave it to
us in powder form. This is going to sting
sir." Mike had the man roll to his right.
He cut the pants again to make the exit
wound more visible. He sprinkled the off
white powder onto the wound before helping
Jerry back over. He poured more into the
wound as the officer winced and moaned in
pain. The medic watched as the bleeding
stopped as the powder solidified. "There we
go sir, bleeding controlled. Just don't
plan on dancing for a while." He joked as
he loosened the tourniquet.

"Shut up Doc," Jerry laughed back as the medic wrapped the wound with the bandage. "No morphine yet Doc," jerry stopped the man as he pulled a small metal syrette from his pack. "Later, I gotta get back into the fight now."

"Ok sir, just be careful. You move too much and you will start bleeding again."

"Roger that. Help me up please Chief." Jerry asked as he grabbed his rifle and held his right arm up. Mike helped the man up before grabbing his pack and running to the next shout for help.

Jerry dropped the empty magazine onto the ground. He reached to pick it up and placed it in an empty pouch on his belt. He grabbed for a magazine he knew he had put away empty to find it filled. He smiled and said a brief prayer of thanks to whatever was orchestrating this before leaning around the large tree and firing into a group of four union soldiers, dropping them all.

Jerry dropped two more union soldiers with aimed shots before pausing to quickly survey the field. He saw three of his men dead and one missing. He assumed something had caused him to disappear like Sergeant Flint. The two heavy guns were slicing through the enemy just like he figured they would. The mortars had taken out all the visible supply and ammo wagons and now targeted large groups of men. He could not see a man in blue above the wall.

The hair on the back of his neck stood and a chill ran through him. He looked around quickly as his hands tightened on his rifle. He spun to the rear as he heard a bugle call sounding the charge. The notes from the brass instrument were close. "Very close," he thought to himself. It only took a moment before a line of Calvary, spread out over fifty yards, came charging through the trees towards him.

"1st Squad, look to your rear!" He shouted as the eight remaining men of the Interdiction teams spun on one knee. Man and beast sprayed the trees red with blood as the Marines opened fire.

"Schanz, take the rear," Sergeant Fisher yelled as he continued walking his weapon around the field to the front. Sergeant Schanz leaped over the log and found the charging horses in the trees. His weapon barked as he killed three horses and wounded five cavalrymen.

Lieutenant Brown heard a scream for a medic to his right. He ran ten paces and found Corporal O'Malley on the ground, a red splotch on the upper right shoulder. Jerry grabbed a bandage from the man's pack and shoved it inside the coat. He pressed hard before the man yelled. "DUCK!" Jerry threw himself down and forward covering the man as he felt a sword slice past where his head was just at. He rolled forward and jumped to his feet. He blocked the next attack with his rifle, parrying the long blade to the left. He released the grip and grabbed the man from the horse, pulling him to the ground. His grey, feathered hat flying off and landing in the dirt. Jerry grabbed his brass knuckles from his jacket pocket as he turned to face the stunned man.

As the man stood Jerry pulled his own sword with his left hand, brass knuckles on his right. The man looked familiar, a Generals star on both shoulders. He knew he had to end this quick since he had never been in a sword fight. The officer circled to Jerry's left and Jerry mimicked the move. The officer swung his sword at Jerry's midsection as he leaped back. The blade halted mid-swing and started back along the same path. Blocking the attack Jerry stepped forward and punched the officer in the face with a glancing blow. The general staggered back three paces as blood dripped from a cut on his left cheek.

Doc Brown ran to the injured man and knelt beside him. He paused, raising his rifle and killing three horsemen riding up at them. He saw his Lieutenant was holding his own so he began to tend to the wounded man.

Jerry took a saber slash to his leg just below the bullet wound. Not very deep, a quick glance told him, but enough to renew the pain. He staggered to the right almost dropping to a knee. The General smiled as he saw the man stumble. He took a step forward and stabbed his sword at the Lieutenant. Jerry spun to avoid the blade and stepped forward grabbing the man's wrist. He pulled him forward and swung his right hand hard. The roundhouse punch, coupled with the brass knuckles made a sickening sound as it crushed the general's cheek. Jerry reached back punched the man twice, as hard and as fast as he could. The first fractured and dislocated the Generals jaw. The second caved in the man's temple. The general's face froze as blood poured from his mouth, the jaw dangling open. He dropped to his knees as Jerry released his grip on the now dead man's wrist. He fell forward with a thud.

Jerry bent over to catch his breath before wiping his bloody brass knuckles off in the thick grass. He stood straight and took three deep breaths. "Nicely done Lieutenant," Doc Brown commented as he looked up from the wounded man he had been treating. "That officer look familiar to you sir?"

"Yes, he did actually. I thought the same thing." Jerry replied as he wrapped a bandage around the fresh wound on his leg. He looked up to see four men riding hard in retreat through the trees. He noticed his men had stopped firing in any direction and took a moment to grab his canteen. He pulled the cork out and took a long pull as Doc Brown walked over to the fallen general. He knelt down and checked for a pulse. Finding none he grabbed the man's coat and rolled him towards him. As the general rolled onto his back the medic stood.

"Damn brass knuckles make a hell of a mess sir," The Chief Petty Officer laughed

as he looked down at the crushed face.
"Holy shit!"

"What is it chief?" Jerry asked after
swallowing another pull from the canteen.
He limped over and looked down at the man
he had killed.

"Sir, this is General George Custer
sir. I did my thesis paper on him in
college."

"Seriously?" Jerry looked trying to
see passed the carnage he created. "Maybe,"
he thought to himself as the medic squatted
down next to the dead man. Jerry rocked
back on his right leg trying to ease the
pain in the other. He grabbed his left
thigh up high as the Doc rummaged through
the general's pockets. He pulled out a few
maps and set them on the ground. Then he
found a tobacco pouch and pipe. These he
tossed to his officer.

"Here you go, sir. Might help take
your mind off the pain," The medic smiled
before continuing the search. A pocket
watch, pencil, and a piece of hardtack all
were placed on top of the maps. "Bingo,"
the man exclaimed as he pulled letter from
the last pocket. He unfolded the yellowed
paper. He took a moment to appreciate the
soft writing on the page, "Obviously a
woman's hand," He spoke to no one before
reading aloud. "My dearest George," he
started and read the one-page letter aloud.
It was full of positive thoughts, praise of
the job he has done and how much he was
missed. "Jesus sir, this thing is full of

sexual innuendos and hidden meanings," the
medic commented after reading the next few
lines in his head first. "It's signed *With
love, your future wife, Libbie*!" The medic
handed the papers over to Jerry.

"Wow," was all the lieutenant could
muster between the pain as he reread the
words.

"Sir, Custer married Elizabeth Bacon
in 1864. Her nickname was Libbie. This
letter is consistent with history as they
often talked about the sexually charged
letters they wrote. Hollywood even made a
few movies about the pair. Her father
refused to let her see him because he came
from a simple background. When he made
Brigadier General her old man had a change
of heart. Once they married she followed
him everywhere."

Jerry folded the letter and put it in
his pocket. Next, he bent down and grabbed
his rifle, dusting it off briefly before
throwing the sling over his shoulder. He
looked down at the fallen general and
thought about all the things he was meant
to do. "Help me back to the line Chief,"
Jerry limped forward as the man tucked the
items from the general in his pack and
stood. He placed Jerry's arm over his
shoulder, grabbing his wrist and helped his
lieutenant a few steps before Jerry stopped
and looked back. "The futures not what it
used to be I guess," he spoke as the two
men began the painful, short journey back
to the squad.

Chapter Twenty One

General's Lee, Pickett, and Longstreet looked up from the table to see an officer riding in hard. The three generals were joined by half a dozen other officers under the large canvas tarp. Four thick hemp ropes keeping it taut in the slight breeze. They returned to the maps on the table for a few moments until the man arrived. The dark brown horse was covered in sweat. The white froth at the corners of its mouth told the officers how hard it had been pushed.

"General Lee sir," The man shouted as he gave a salute from atop the steed. "Lieutenant Davison, General Ewell's division."

"Yes Davison, report," Lee ordered in his slow southern drawl, as he removed his hat to wipe the sweat from his brow with a handkerchief. The heat of the day mixed with the heavy linen and wool uniforms made the weather stifling, but a southern officer did have a reputation to live up to.

The man dismounted and approached. "Sirs, that new unit you sent has been wreaking havoc amongst the blue bellies. Their weapons reach out farther than the Union guns, and they do not miss sir." The man's voice held a mixture of fear and respect. "Their cannons have destroyed every stockpile within sight, and their sharpshooters kill two or three at a shot sir."

"That's impossible Lieutenant." Longstreet fired back as he removed his hat.

"General I would agree if I had not witnessed this myself. They used long guns and some type of cannon first. They cut down men like a scythe through wheat. The Union soldiers hid behind the rock wall and none of them will approach the remaining cannon for love or money sir." The man paused to take a deep swig from his canteen. The General moved two full Corp against them, had to be close to 800 men in total and they killed every last one."

General Lee looked hard at the man, "Major Peterson said he had a total of 80 men. How is this possible?" He asked the officer.

"Sir, whatever kind of rifle they are using, I have never seen the like. They can shoot twenty or thirty shots at a time. They are not muskets sir. And they are nothing like the repeating rifles the Union Calvary carry. They have three or for giant rifles that feed the ammo using a belt-like thing." The man took a second drink before General Pickett offered him a flask. "God bless you, General." The man spoke before taking a swig from the flask, grimacing slightly as he handed it back, his throat full of a welcome fire. "General Lee, I

have never before seen the firepower these
men bring, sir."

"What is General Meade doing through
all this, I wonder?" General Lee spoke as
he turned to look at the table.

"General Meade looks to have pulled
six more Corp from throughout his lines
sir. They were fast marching them in as I
rode to report. He also brought in two more
artillery units but those were destroyed
before they could unhook them from the
horses. General Ewell's Division is firing
their cannon at the enemy to keep them
behind the wall but waiting for any orders
before moving forward."

"That explains the movement to the
rear our scouts have been reporting from
across the battlefield sir." General
Longstreet offered.

"Sir, the enemy started a barrage of
cannon fire early against General Ewell's
unit but it stopped as soon as the new unit
opened fire. We did not take any casualties
as of yet. It seems General Meade is moving
his units to support the east side of the
battlefield from this unit's firepower.
However, General Ewell reports his men are
ready to charge up Culp's Hill and take it,
Sir."

"Lieutenant, I want you to ride back
along the lines tell every General to
attack and move forward. I will give you
one hour to return to General Ewell and
then I will send General Longstreet's

entire Division across the field. We will continue the artillery barrage as they move, but with Ewell's Division and Major Peterson's unit we should draw their attention east and give General Pickett a good chance on his march." General Lee turned and walked to the opposite side of the table. He removed his hat, the large white feather standing straight up as he sat it on the map. "Generals, any suggestions?"

"No sir," General Longstreet offered first. "I think we have a better chance now than ever before. The Union will not expect a full-frontal assault along the whole line. It sounds like this unit of special troops has forced Meade to move his troops from their desired positions. If we can catch a few in transit, we might throw the whole Army of the Potomac into chaos."

"I agree, General," Pickett added. "This is the perfect opportunity and my men are eager for a fight sir."

General Lee looked at the map as his officers stood awaiting their orders. Next, he stepped outside the tent, forgetting his hat on the table. He looked across the wide-open field, smoke from both sides drifting in the light breeze. Looking to the row of houses that sat on the faraway hilltop, he wiped his brow again. "This is the place," He thought to himself, "This field, this hill, this sacred ground. Dear Lord, protect my men as they battle the enemy." He sent the silent prayer up to his maker. Lee's back became stiff, "God's will," he finally spoke aloud before turning. "Lieutenant," he spoke, turning to face the officers.

"Sir," The man took a half step forward.

"Ride hard, give the General's my orders with my compliments if you please! Full attack at 1300 hours."

"Yes Sir," the man shouted as he gave a quick salute. He mounted a fresh horse that a Sergeant held and took off reaching a gallop within a hundred feet.

"Generals ready your men. Longstreet cut the artillery to half shots till Pickett's men move. Then pour it on with great vigor!" Lee put his hat back on his head. "Gentlemen," this is our day and our battlefield. I believe God wants us to win this fight and I have total faith in you and the men. Now fight hard for the SOUTH!"

The gathered officers stood to attention as one and saluted. Each held a smile on his face and turned to head off to their units. "God's will," Lee repeated as the horses rode away and he looked once again across the smoke covered field.

Chapter Twenty-two

"Jerry, you ok?" Major Peterson asked as he saw Doc Brown helping the injured officer.

"Yes Sir got in a sword fight, would you believe." The man smiled as the doc sat him on an ammo crate.

"Hold still sir and let me stitch this up quick before you go and bleed out."

"Yes Chief," Jerry smiled back as the medic removed the quickly placed bandage from his leg. Tearing the pant leg open he got a better look at the wound.

"Damn swords cut deep, but it doesn't look like he cut anything major." The man spoke as he poured alcohol on the wound making Lieutenant Brown wince in pain.

"Damn doc that hurts."

"Well, sir I leave it up to you. Either I stitch this up as is and you charge the hill, or I give you some morphine, stitch it up all nice and pretty and you're out of the fight for a few hours?"

"Gee thanks Chief." He gritted his teeth, "have at it Doc." He said as his hands grasped the sides of the crate in anticipation of the coming pain.

Mark walked closer to look for himself. "Sergeant?" He yelled to the mortar teams. "Looks like they have no more supply wagons that aren't burning. Start taking down the wall. One team fire at the far edge nearest Culp's Hill lets soften them up for Ewell's Division. The other start on our left flank and make the enemy pull back further. The third mortar, give them ten minutes to bunch up in the middle then bring that down as well."

"Copy that Major," the sergeant in charge yelled back. The two fire teams made quick corrections on their tubes and began sending rounds downrange.

Mark looked at his Lieutenant's leg and smiled. "Chicks dig scars, Jerry."

"That's what they say, Major," Jerry smiled back. "Shit!" he exclaimed as the Doc pushed the needle through at the inside of the thigh to start his repairs.

Mark was joined by Captain Pike as the first rounds hit to the left. The pair watched as the wall exploded, sending rocks and men in all directions. They pulled the binoculars to their eyes as the second rounds hit. A plume of smoke, blood, rubble, and meat rose quickly. Those men that could, crawled or ran away in fear, falling over one another.

150

Brian turned to watch the opposite fire mission have the same effect. When the wall exploded, he heard a loud cheer go up from General Ewell's men posted just outside the tree line. Rebels stood and waved their hats in the air as the mortar teams disintegrated the protective wall. The second and third blast caught a large group of men moving to fill a gap in the lines and killed twenty men in a flash.

Mark motioned for First and second squad to pull back and watched as they reentered the tree line. Pulling his pipe from the inside of his coat, he filled the bowl with tobacco and lit it with a match. He took several short puffs to help the tobacco catch before taking a long draw. He closed his eyes, letting the smoke dance around in his mouth before exhaling it into the air, the breeze pulled it to his right. He continued to enjoy his pipe as his snipers continued to shoot. "Take a break, boys! let the mortars do the work for now. Rehydrate and smoke 'em if you got 'em," He ordered before taking another draw on his own pipe.

Brian came close and pulled his pocket watch from his vest. "12:30 Major. We've done a fair bit of killing before lunch." Brian smiled as he lit the cigar he pulled out.

"Yes we have my friend," he almost smiled before remembering what they were doing. "Hate to say it but these soldiers never had a chance. Casualties?"

"Minor," Brian replied as he exhaled his smoke into the air. "Third and fourth squads are intact. Only their snipers are engaged."

"First squad has four dead and seven injured including me Sir," Jerry gritted out from between his clenched teeth. "None of the injuries are major sir. All injured can still fight or will fight when the medics are done with them. Two of the four dead have vanished, sir." He smiled briefly before the needle pierced his thigh again.

"All medics are accounted for Major." Doc Brown reported as he continued to sew the wound.

"76 men remaining, seven of those injured," Mark spoke out loud to the battlefield. Mark continued to smoke his pipe as he looked along the edges of the field. The sounds of nearby rifle fire and the pressure waves of the mortars mixed with the distant screams of the wounded and scared enemy. "Jerry can you make the march across the field?"

"Yes sir, I won't be doing any running but I can grunt through it. Right, Doc?" He asked as he looked to his medic.

"Yeah, you can make it. Gonna hurt like hell though. And if you try and run you're going to rip these stitches and then I am gonna be pissed." He smiled at the officer.

"Ok, as soon as you're fixed I want you to combine first and second squad and await new orders."

"Copy that sir," He replied quickly as what he hoped was the last time the needle entered his flesh.

Brian and Mark reached for their pistols as a horse surprised them from the right.

"Sirs," the mounted man snapped a salute. "With General Lee's compliments." The man moved his hand back down to the reigns. "You are ordered to start a full attack and forward charge at 1300 hours."

"Copy that Lieutenant," Mark replied with a return salute. "Be safe and God's speed son." He finished as the man turned his horse and galloped off.

"Ok, Men, we have our orders. We attack in two-five minutes. Alert the men and have them ready everything. Mortar teams will continue to soften the walls and then walk the fire forward as the men approach. Have Team Two support the infantry on our right. Switch to wagons and large groups until we march, then have them finish destroying the walls."

Roger that Major," Brian saluted as he dropped his cigar and stamped it out with his boot. He headed to the mortar teams and gave them their orders. Team two quickly disassembled their mortar and moved it a hundred yards to the right, to give the confederate infantry better coverage.

Doc Brown finished bandaging the Lieutenant's leg. There you go sir, remember, no running." He gave the order with a smile washing his hands from his canteen before taking a long pull of the tepid fluid.

"Thanks, Doc," Jerry patted the man on the shoulder as he picked up his rifle and limped towards his men.

"Major," Doc Brown spoke as he stood. "If you don't mind I will stay with the new first squad and send my other two medics with the second?"

"Good idea Chief, give the word and prepare for battle," Mark ordered as Chief Petty Officer Brown picked up his own rifle and headed to inform the medics of the new task.

"Major?" Brian asked returning.

"Brian let's advance with the men. Have the mortar teams post their own rear security. We will leave four men each to man the mortars. We will also bring the snipers with us and let them set up closer to the fighting. With the whole Confederate lines moving the distraction should give them an open field to shoot from. That means we will be moving forward with about 50 Marines in total. Hitting the hill with 44, barring no casualties if we are lucky."

154

"Sounds about right sir," Brian replied. "What's wrong sir?"

"Hmm?" Mark caught by surprise at the question. "Oh nothing really, that just doesn't sound like many men against a few thousand spread along their lines."

"You're right to worry Mark," Brian moved closer to his friend. "But remember we have more firepower in each of those men than thirty or forty of the enemy soldiers. Plus, I think after the destruction of those 800 men they sent that the enemy will run scared when they see us approaching. We got this Major!"

"You're right Brian." Mark replied after a moment of thought, "Thanks buddy, I needed that!" He turned to his second in command. "Now let's go kick some Blue Belly ass!"

Chapter Twenty Three

General Meade and his staff looked from the porch of his cabin, mouths hanging wide open. He could not believe his eyes. "800 men, all gone in a matter of minutes." His voice breaking as he spoke the words.

"General, who are these soldiers?" One of his officers asked. "The firepower…unbelievable." The man let his head drop as his mouth went dry.

Meade took out binoculars to try and get a better view of the lines. He watched as men coward behind the rock walls. None of his soldiers dare look above it for fear of being the next target of sharpshooters. He blessed the brief moments without an explosion. But the blessing was short-lived as the silence was shattered when the rock wall to his right exploded, taking five men and horse with it. Two more explosions sent men and rock flying through the air, those closest to them scrambling to fall back. They left their muskets and ran. Those who could not run clawed their way back and were trampled by those who could run. More explosions began on his left as the wall nearest Culp's Hill began to disintegrate in front of his men. "I hear no firing of cannon, only smoke from inside the tree line. What kind of cannon fires without report?"

"I have no idea, sir," one aide answered as the gathered saw their front line disintegrate and become a general retreat.

Three riders arrived in unison, "Sir," one saluted. General Hancock reports a full-frontal attack. That made the staff turn. "He reports massive artillery fire has recommenced. He says ten thousand plus men are advancing on Cemetery Ridge."

"General Meade," the next shouted without a salute. "General Briney reports the same from just north of Little Round Top."

The third had dismounted, "General Slocum has the same report from all sides of Culp's Hill."

Meade quickly lifted his binoculars and looked to the far right of the line where the soundless cannons had been firing. He watched as a few men stood and exited the tree line and began moving forward. He walked his view left to see a large infantry force exit from the trees to the southernmost edge of Culp's Hill.

A massive explosion made the group rush around the building to the western side. Half of Meade's artillery had been destroyed in a single barrage. "Captain," he looked to the man on his left. "Go find out what that was." The man grabbed the nearest empty stead and rode off. He watched as the confederate artillery, easily ¾ of a mile away was enveloped with

smoke as the cannons fired. The firing
paused briefly as a line of soldiers exited
the smoke, marching on his positions.

"I said yesterday they would attack
from that direction, but what is Lee doing
attacking along the entire front?" Meade
asked the air. "This is not like General
Lee at all." His question was drowned out
as his remaining artillery opened fire on
the advancing troops. The first salvo was
short but they were ready for when the
advancing troop reached that line.

Musket fire opened up behind him as he
rushed back to the eastern side. The
advancing troops had made up a lot of
ground and were now taking cover behind
what was left of the rock wall. His junior
officers were trying to put up a defense,
having their men take cover behind the
wooden post wall they had rapidly built as
a fallback position over the last 2 days.
It wasn't much, thin tree trunks set at
angles to each other and only about 2 feet
high. The men were trying to fire back but
if the ball rounds from the enemy didn't go
in between the gaps it struck wood and sent
shrapnel into his men. The mysterious
troops on his right flank were in view. He
lifted his binoculars and focused on a few
of them. Their uniforms were odd and their
weapons were unlike anything he had ever
seen. They fired multiple rounds without
having to reload. When they did pause they
didn't load from the barrel but just
replaced a box in the bottom of the weapon
and rapidly began firing again.

A group of three Union privates and a sergeant had stacked up in the "V" where the wood fence was joined and was trying to hit the approaching enemy. He saw an enemy soldier lift his rifle; it had a large round tube hooked to the bottom. The soldier held the gun at waist height and grabbed the box at the bottom. Meade saw a small flash of smoke before seeing the four men evaporate in an explosion. The fence now held only a gaping hole, the fractured ends covered in blood and sinew. "Mother of God," the General exclaimed as he let his binoculars drop.

The enemy soldier moved the tube forward and Meade watched as a metal case dropped out. The man placed something back in the tube and aimed it at the General and his staff. "GET DOWN!" he yelled as he flung himself forward. His cabin behind him exploded as the force sent him flying hard forward with increased momentum. Meade rolled a few times before stopping. He sat up, ears ringing, the sounds of the battle slowly increased as his senses returned.

"General? Are you alright sir?" The major kneeling in front of him asked. The man took a handkerchief from his pocket and held it against the General's head. "You're bleeding sir." The major spoke as he held the cloth against the Generals head to staunch the bleeding.

"I am alright Major, thank you," Meade replied as he took control of the cloth and stood uneasily. "What the hell was that?"

"It looked like a portable cannon of some type sir. I have never heard of such a thing." One lieutenant asked as Meade looked to see his cabin destroyed and the remnants burning.

"General," Meade turned to see the Captain he had sent to check on his artillery. "II Corp moved their artillery to discourage the attack at Cemetery Ridge. The enemy cannon fire made a lucky shot and destroyed close to half of the cannon battery before they were ready to fire."

"What is the status of the remaining artillery?" Meade asked quickly as he looked in all directions on the battlefield. He paused briefly as his eyes locked on the makeshift hospital they had created in two of the barns on the property they occupied. Several tents were set up in a line to give the wounded men cover after any needed surgery was performed within the barns. A bad taste entered his mouth as he remembered the pile of amputated body parts he saw behind the barns the night before. The barns and the tents were now overflowing with wounded. Never before had he seen such carnage from a battle.

"General Hunt stated he will…" The man would never finish the sentence as Meade turned in time to have his aide's face explode onto his from a sharpshooter's bullet. The sticky sweet warm blood covered the general's face. Meade wiped the blood from his eyes only to become frozen by the sight of the man's corpse standing before him. A large hole remained where his face

should be, the body standing for another
moment before falling straight down, his
legs giving out on their former owner. The
general vomited down the front of his
uniform before he knew it.

"General?" The officer's voice broke
as he looked at his leader. He wasn't sure
if the man was hurt until the General
spoke.

"Yes," Meade finally able to speak as
he frantically washed the blood from his
face with a canteen of water.

"Sir, the confederates have taken
Cemetery Hill."

"What?" The general stopped cleaning
himself and finally realized that General
Howard stood before him. "General Howard?"
Meade asked in disbelief.

"Sir, the confederate infantry overran
my lines. They are now digging in before
advancing further. I lost over half my
force, sir. Over half of MY MEN dead,
injured, or captured." The general reported
with embarrassment. "We pulled back to here
but the entire northern line is collapsing
sir."

"My God," Meade exclaimed as he tried
to grasp the new development.

Chapter Twenty Four

Major General George Pickett led his men from the front. His was the first of three divisions making their way across the open fields towards the Northern Army lines that spread out across Cemetery ridge. They were receiving sporadic artillery fire and the occasional canister round but nothing near what he had expected.

The men were approaching the Angle, a low rock wall that acted as the first line for the enemy. Pickett had his men stop a hundred feet shy of the wall and prepare to fire. The union soldiers fired first, forty men in the front of his lines fell. The rebel soldiers in the front line took a knee as the second line moved up between them. "Ready," General Pickett raised his sword. "Aim!" He shouted as the enemy soldiers rushed to reload their muskets. "Fire," he shouted as the wall and soldiers disappeared behind the musket smoke. His men reloaded as the breeze carried the cloud away. When they were preparing to shoot a second volley Pickett watched as the Northern line broke.

A few random soldiers turned and shot wildly as they ran east. The front lines fired a second volley at the running soldiers. "Forward men!" Pickett ordered as the men stood and climbed over the wall. As they crossed the wall they found over a hundred dead or wounded Union soldiers.

"Where are all the enemy soldiers?" Pickett asked the Captain to his left.

"Sir I have no idea. This morning this wall was full, two to three deep in sections with the blue bellies." The captain replied as he shrugged his shoulders. "I am not one to complain though sir," He smiled briefly.

"I have to agree sir," Pickett replied with a smile in his deep Virginia drawl. The men continued to move forward as the sounds of cannons started to taper off.

General Meade stood on the hill speechless, watching as his men surrendered. The Union soldiers stood and spun their muskets so they could hold them high in the air by the barrels.

"General Meade sir?" The man turned to see a Major standing in a strange Confederate uniform, behind him stood a Captain. "Sir, Major Mark Peterson and Captain Brian Pike, Confederate Marines." The Captain held his rifle tight to his shoulder, with the barrel pointed down. It was unlike any rifle he had ever seen. His mind spun as he watched more of the oddly dressed soldiers round up his men within his sight.

"Sir, you are now my prisoner, please hand me your sword and pistol." Meade stood looking across his camp as he heard the words. His hand dropped to his waist and began to slowly unbuckle his belt, the smell of his vomit made him gag briefly as the severity of his losses made their way through the fog in his head.

"Major Peterson," Meade's voice broke at first before becoming stronger. "Allow me to send word to my commanders to cease-fire and surrender in place."

"Of Course General," Mark agreed as he took the offered belt with the Generals weapons attached.

"Lieutenant," Meade ordered to the man on his left as he watched the junior officer hand over his sword and pistol. "Send riders to all units. Ceasefire immediately and surrender your weapons." General Meade let his shoulders drop at the words.

Brian dropped his weapon, letting it hang by the linen sling. Brian grabbed two chairs and brought them towards the two officers now standing under a tree. "Gentleman," he sat the chairs in the shade.

"Thank you, Captain," Peterson offered as he motioned the General to one of the chairs. "General if you please?"

"Thank you, Major," Meade replied as he fell into the chair, the stress of the last few hours bleeding away. Mark offered the man a cigar and lit it for him. Next he filled his pipe and joined the General. "Major, where did your unit come from? Your clothes, your weapons, like nothing I have ever dreamed of."

"We are a small tactical unit. We have been researching the weapons we use for years." Mark offered trying to stay a little vague with how.

"Your accent, you are not a southern gentleman sir." The general smiled.

"Born in the south, raised in the north, sir." Mark took a deep draw from his pipe as he watched the Generals mind race.

"Major Peterson, sir?" Mark turned his head to see Lieutenant Brown at attention and saluting. He returned the salute lightly. "Sir we have secured the camp. Doc Brown and his medics have treated the few wounded we suffered and are now assisting with any wounded soldier they find. "I had Sergeant Klomp pack the wagons with the mortars and ammo. He should be up here in a few minutes."

The men all turned as General Ewell approached on his horse. "Lieutenant, have the men prepare to move back to camp as soon as possible," Mark ordered as the General dismounted. He stood to greet the General. "General Ewell," Mark stood and saluted the man. "Here are the General's weapons." Mark offered the belt with sword and pistol attached.

General Ewell took the belt and looked
at it for a moment. "Major, this belongs to
you and your men. You took this hill and
the Generals staff. Thank you though sir
for the respect you have shown." The man
slightly bowed as he handed Mark the
weapons back.

Mark took the belt, pride showing
brightly on his face. He pulled out his
pocket watch and saw that it was only four
o'clock. "Not a bad days work," he smiled
to himself. "With your permission, I will
gather my men and return to our camp."

"Permission granted Major. You and
your men have earned the respite." The
general returned Marks salute crisply.
"General Meade, I am General Ewell sir."
Mark heard the man say as he met up with
Brian and the pair walked off to gather the
men. Sergeant Sutton had gathered the
horses and brought four of them up to the
Major and Captain. Doc Brown helped
Lieutenant Brown get up on his horse before
stepping into his horse's stirrup and
lifting himself up and over the back of his
horse. They quickly made their way to the
rest of the men and led them back to the
tree line. Once the men had loaded the
wagons with wounded men and materials they
made their way back towards their camp. As
they left they watched General Lee and
Longstreet approaching the former Union
Command post.

Chapter Twenty Five

The wounded were placed in the medical tent and Doc Brown was double-checking their wounds. "Excellent work, Men!" Mark bellowed as they finished unloading the wagons. "Brian, let's get security teams set up. The rest of you deserve a rest. Mr. Engleman think you can lite the fires and give us a hearty meal?"

"Yes sir," Doug replied as he pointed to two of the men to help him.

"Excellent, clean your weapons and then yourselves boys," Mark ordered before turning to head into the command tent. Once inside he walked to the potbelly stove in the corner. Kneeling down he opened the door and shoved in a few sticks and some wood shavings before lighting it with a match. He stared into the blackness and watched as the fire took hold, slowly dancing across the shavings and lighting the bigger sticks. When those had caught hold he filled the space with a few even bigger chunks before shutting the door.

Captain Pike walked in and saw what his friend was doing. He grabbed the pot of cold coffee from breakfast and walked outside to dump it. He took a couple of cups of water from the barrel out front and rinsed the old grounds out before refilling it with fresh water. Walking back in, he

set it on top of the stove and grabbed the
bag of already crushed coffee grounds from
the table nearby. He dumped a handful into
the pot and replaced the cover. "Well sir,
that went better than expected I think."
Brian smiled as Mark stood from lighting
the fire.

"I think your right," Mark said in a
faded voice as he went out front to fill a
basin with water from the same barrel Brian
had used. He walked back in and set the
basin on the table. He moved the maps to
the far end. "I honestly can't believe I
actually met General Meade." Mark smiled as
he removed his coat and vest, setting them
on top of the maps. "I wonder," He paused
briefly as he splashed the cold refreshing
water on his face. "How many lives we may
have saved in the end?" He finished before
lifting two more handfuls up to his face.

"I am not sure sir," Brian replied as
he entered with his own basin. His coat and
vest he hung on the back of a nearby chair
before just shoving his face down into the
basin and leaving it there for a few
seconds. When he came back up he stepped
back and brushed the water through his
short hair. The dirt and smoke draining off
his head as the water flowed down. Both men
rolled up the sleeves on their linen shirts
and washed their hands and arms, happy to
feel the sweat and heat from the day being
cleaned off. Their bodies cooling in the
breeze as it flowed stronger through the
open flaps of the tent.

Both men loosened their shirts by unbuttoning the top few buttons and walked outside. Mark lit his pipe and then Brian's cigar with a wooden match. A quick look showed two security teams had been set up a few meters outside the camp. Several men had stripped down to the underwear and were enjoying the cold water of the river at the edge of the camp. The near waist-high water being splashed around by the men like kids at a community pool. Brian closed his eyes and smiled as the smell of meat cooking passed through the air from the cook tent.

Lieutenant Stevens approached and offered a salute, "Sirs, I figured it would be ok to give some of the men a break. I have teams already on security and will change them out once the men get some food."

"Good idea Dave. You and your men did a great job today by the way." Mark replied returning the salute. "Please pass along my compliments to them."

"I will sir, thank you, sir."

"What are your thoughts on today's battle Lieutenant?" Mark asked.

"Honestly sir it could not have gone better. Captain Pike's idea to start early with the long guns had a demoralizing effect that was visible right away sir. Add to that the destruction of those two regiments they sent towards us. From the sounds of it we galvanized fighting along the entire front before General Lee gave the order to charge." The man paused as he took a drink of coffee offered to him by Captain Pike. "Thank you, sir," he said as he carefully blew onto the cup before sampling.

The three officers stood silently for a few moments enjoying the hot brew and listening to the men as they relaxed from the day's battle. Lt Stevens continued, "Our wounded are all doing well according to the doc. We have 3 dead and 3 missing, one each from the last fight up to the hill. We searched extensively for the bodies but several men report seeing them disappear." He stopped briefly to send up a prayer for them. "Lieutenant Brown is resting in the medical tent, Doc Brown gave him some morphine to combat the pain." He smiled again as he took another drink from the steaming cup. "All ammo has been refilled, which is a good thing and we brought all spare ammo crates back with us."

"Excellent thank you, Dave, now go relax a bit," Mark ordered as he took a drag from his pipe.

"Thank you, sir, I will go join the men in the river and wash the dirt off." He laughed as he saluted and turned on his heels.

"Well Mark, we captured the Army of the Potomac and General Meade. Poor guy was only in command for five days." Brian smirked. "I wonder what General Hooker and General Halleck will say when they find

out. At this point, General Hooker is not
the overall leader of the Northern Army
right?"

"No Brian, you are right, he is still
commander in the West. But he is in
Vicksburg fighting at the same time as us.
He didn't take over the Union Army till
1864." Mark spoke pulling the memory from
his college days. "I am thinking we may
need to fight at least one more battle to
prove to the North what they are being
told," Mark replied before finishing his
coffee and turning to refill his cup.

General Lee stood under the makeshift
tent his men had prepared for him next to
the demolished house on the hilltop used by
General Meade. His commanders stood around
the table made from sawhorses and planks of
wood. Smiles were plastered on their faces.
"Gentleman how stands the Army?" Lee asked.

General Longstreet stood upright, "Sir
we have 150 dead and double that wounded
from Pickett's charge sir. That is a lot
less than we had planned for this morning,
sir." All the gathered men nodded in
agreement before he continued. "We have
finished rounding up all the men of the
Army of the Potomac. The general staff has
been placed under guard in a barn about two
miles south of us. The rest of the men are
being guarded at various points around the
battlefield." He showed the officers with
small wooden blocks placed on the map.
"Weapons and ammo have been gathered and
distributed to the regiments to supplement
what they have. There is some food that

made it through the battle that was stored
in barns on the far side away from Major
Peterson's men." He paused to smile,
"Whatever was in sight they seemed to
destroy sir."

Lee paused to look back at the
foundation that remained to prove that
point. "Very true General," General Lee
laughed, "please continue."

"We have enough food for two days to
feed all the men on both sides, sir. We
will need to resupply quickly or figure out
what to do with all the prisoners' sir."
Longstreet paused for a moment before
continuing. We were able to capture about
60 cannons intact sir, most of the rounds
unfired. One artillery officer said they
were waiting for orders to open fire when
we came up the field. But those orders
never came. I do not have any totals on
dead and wounded yet for either side sir
but I do have my junior officers traveling
around the battlefield to find out. I
should have good numbers by six o'clock.
Also all officers have been ordered to
treat the prisoners well. Our doctors also
have been ordered to give care to the
wounded."

"Very well general, thank you." Lee
paused to look at the map. He couldn't help
but smile at the markers showing his men in
command of so many Union prisoners. "I want
a courier sent immediately to President
Davis. Inform him of our victory and the
surrender of the Army of the Potomac. Also,
send riders to General's Johnson and Cooper

informing them of the same and ask if they need re-enforcements."

"Yes sir," a faceless voice replied before turning and walking out from under the tarp.

"Gentleman the men have earned a well-needed rest. We will stay here a few days while we wait for a reply from the President. General Stuart?" The Calvary General moved forward to the table having finally arrived after the battle with his men. "I want you to organize foraging parties. Send some men to find our supply wagons as well as anything edible to give to the men."

General Jeb Stuart looked perplexed at the orders. "Sir shouldn't I…"

"General I do not know what kept you from this battle but I want you to help now that it's over." Lee looked straight into the man's eyes. The subordinate wilted slightly before turning.

"Yes sir," He saluted crisply before leaving. The gathered officers were surprised seeing how Stuart was always Lee's favorite. General Longstreet let a smile pass briefly at the turn of events.

Lee turned briefly, "Orderly?" He yelled and a man approached with a tray full of glasses. Each was half full of brown liquor. "Gentleman let us drink to our victory," Lee ordered as the glasses were passed out. "VICTORY!"

"VICTORY," all the officers shouted,
lifting their glasses before draining them
in one pull.

"God's will," Lee spoke softly before
draining his glass.

Chapter Twenty-Six

General Hooker and his men were
gathered outside under a tarp to escape the
heat that sweltered inside the cabin he was
using as his command post. They had stopped
for the night just south of Harper's Ferry,
West Virginia. He was headed back to
Washington after resigning his command.
Even at midnight, the heat was stifling.
The gathered officers were worried by the
reports they were receiving from the few
men who managed to escape the battle at
Gettysburg. Hooker continued to stare at
the map. "We had won the first two days,"
he thought to himself as his finger traced
from Union location to union location.

The general finally looked up as the
rider approached; he was not riding full
tilt but walked his horse up till just
outside the tent. Both man and beast were
covered in sweat from the hard ride they
had endured. He slowly dismounted and
approached the command staff. "General,"
the man saluted briefly, "Message from
General Meade sir." He handed the note to a
nearby colonel who then handed it to
General Hooker.

Hooker opened the yellow paper and
read the brief note. His command staff
stunned to silence as the blood left the

commanders face. "Captain, is this accurate?" He asked in disbelief to the messenger.

"Yes sir," the Captain replied meekly, "I was there sir. General Lee asked me to deliver this personally so I could verify its contents."

"Gentlemen," Hooker spoke after gathering his thoughts, "General Meade has surrendered his army." Hooker took a drink from a nearby canteen.

It took several minutes before any of the officers could speak. "Sir, how was this possible?" A Colonel finally asked.

"Captain?" Hooker spoke to the man who brought the news. "What happened?" The officers stood frozen as the man gave a description of the day's events. General Hooker lit a cigar and sat in a chair as he listened to the report. It took twenty minutes to report on everything that had occurred. A large portion of it was describing the devastation the Army had received at the hands of the special troops and weapons and Meade's attempt to combat this group. He told of the troop movements used to combat this force and how that weakened the remaining lines causing them to fall as well. He finished with the appearance of this mysterious force and their charge on the flank. "General Lee sent this message to the entire Union Command staff sir."

"He wants everyone to know of this Southern victory," Hooker said to the gathered officers.

The gathered officers turned slowly to look at the leader as the story ended. The captain took a long pull from his canteen to combat the dry mouth that accompanied the retelling of the massacre. Hooker closed his eyes as he drew from the cigar. "Orderly!" He commanded; "bring me my notebook and pencil." A Sargent appeared and handed the items to the General before disappearing from under the tarp.

"Gentlemen, I am writing to the President to let him know of today's events. I am also asking for his instructions, however, can someone tell me how the Southerners have developed such weapons?" The gathered men stood with blank expressions. "We have the Sharps repeater, the Gatling Gun, yet from what the Captain says these are peashooters compared to their weapons." He stopped writing for a moment to draw on the cigar once again. "Someone pour me a drink please."

A surprised Colonel poured three fingers of whiskey into a glass and handed it to his General. Hooker took the offered glass with a nod and drank half of it in one gulp. Letting the liquid burn his throat as he savored the flavor with his eyes closed.

"How many men did we lose?" Hooker asked as he opened his eyes to look to his commanders.

"Sir," the Captain who delivered the note took a step forward, "We had roughly 94,000 Men on the battlefield. I watched as at least 4000 were killed on our flank. And three times that wounded. I am unsure how many escaped but the confederates were still bringing in totals to General Lee when I left. At last count, we had 40,000 captured and half that dead or injured by the reports I overheard, Sir." The Captain's face went pale as he added up the numbers in his head and finally gave a total to all he heard.

"How long did it take you to find us?" Hooker asked as he finished the whiskey.

The captain looked at his watch in the firelight and it showed ten minutes after midnight. "Sir, it took me 10 hours of hard riding to find your camp."

"Thank you, Captain," he spoke as he turned to a Major near the table. "Find this man a tent and let him get some sleep. Here," Hooker handed the Captain a full bottle of whiskey, "This will help you calm down." The officer saluted and turned on his heels, almost falling over from the exhaustion he felt.

The gathered commanders stood in silence as Hooker set his notebook on the table, poured himself a second glass and finished writing a two-page letter. "Colonel Jefferson?"

"Sir!" The man stepped forward.

"You are to ride to Washington and put
this in the hands of either the Secretary
of Defense or the President himself; no one
else Colonel. Tell them of the story you
just heard from the Captain and await
instructions."

"Yes sir," the officer saluted and
tucked the note inside his coat before
stepping out from the tent and ordering his
horse to be brought. Hooker sipped his
drink as a Captain and 2 sergeants joined
the Colonel for the ride North.

Chapter Twenty Seven

Mark stood outside the command tent with a cup of hot coffee in his hands. He watched as the sun rose and started to break through the trees.

"Good Morning Major," he heard Brian Pike's voice to his right.

He turned to see his captain, coffee in hand, cigar in his mouth and his shirt un-tucked and unbuttoned. "Casual today Brian?" Mark laughed.

"Yes sir, it is too hot to go full wool this morning." He smiled back as they both took a sip of the hot brew.

"Approved," Mark spoke as he set the cup on a nearby stump and reached for his pipe. "Let's let the men sleep in today. They earned it." He gave the order in between filling and lighting his pipe.

"Roger that. It's 0630 and the last guard change was at 0400 so they should be fine." The two men switched between coffee and tobacco as they listened to the clanging in the cook tent to their left. They were beginning to smell bacon as it was being prepared for the men. Brian tossed the butt of his cigar in a nearby campfire before continuing. "So what now Sir?" He asked.

"Good question Captain," Mark replied with a smile as he tapped his pipe on his boot heel to dislodge the burnt remnants. "I am guessing we should hear from the General this morning and it will be up to him. But for now, we rest, heal and relax. We have no idea what the world will be like anymore. This is our new past."

The men slowly awoke and walked from their tents as the smell of the food carried throughout the camp. Everyone was in great spirits as the day passed slowly by. Tasks were completed without gripes, smiles never left a face for long and the men all enjoyed the rest day.

Around noon, Lieutenant Brown limped from the medical tent with a crutch under his arm. "Hey Jerry, how is ya feeling?" Brian asked as he saw the man first.

"Did I ever tell you how nice morphine is?" he smiled as he sat on an ammo crate just outside the command tent. The gathered officers laughed as one of them handed him a cup of coffee. "Doc Brown re-stitched the wound last night and ordered me to stay in bed till now. He warned me yesterday I would tear the stitches but I didn't listen." He smiled again as he drank. "How are the men?"

Mark just waved his hand around the camp as Jerry's eyes followed. He smiled as he saw the men were in good spirits. "I figured, that was a hell of a battle yesterday gentlemen."

"Yes, it was," Brian replied. "Could not have asked for it to go better.

"Rider approaching!" They heard a sentry call out as the officers looked in the direction it came from. They watched as a Captain rode up with two sergeants. The Captain jumped from his horse as it skidded to a stop.

"Major, From General Longstreet sir," the man handed a yellow piece of folder paper over before saluting and remounting his horse.

Major Peterson fired back a salute and watched the riders leave before opening the papers. He read through them as 6 more officers approached having seen the riders.

"Gentlemen this is the butcher's bill from the battle. According to General Longstreet, the North had approximately 94,000 men. We have captured 42,450 alive, 21,562 dead or injured. The rest are believed to have evaded capture and escaped."

"Jesus!" One of the gathered officers exclaimed.

"That's a lot of men to try and control Major." Another voiced his thoughts.

Mark continued "We had approximately 72,000 men. The general reports 7,149 dead and 6,285 injured."

"That's half of what we were taught," Brian spoke up as Mark took a breath.

"General Lee is sending the commanders of the Northern Armies a message to come and get their dead and wounded from the battlefield. He states he will pull his men back as they approach and promises to not engage the northern armies while they do this." Mark looked at the officers. "Well we wondered if we made a difference. According to this we surely did." He smiled at the officers and saw both pride and disbelief in their eyes at the butcher's bill.

The officers all saluted before leaving and spreading the news to the rest of the camp. High fives and handshakes were exchanged by the Marines as they got the news. The hours passed as the men enjoyed the relaxing day, hot thought it was. As the men from the sentry post were exchanged at the 1800 hour mark three wagons approached with the same riders who delivered the casualties list.

As the wagons approached the men all gathered near the command tent, each holding a weapon in the case. The wagons came to a stop just short of the command tent. Four were full of beautiful women, dressed in flowing, ankle-length dresses with hats and big bows on their heads. The brilliant blues, reds, and yellows of their fabric a stark contrast to anything seen in the camp. They all smiled and waved at the Marines as the men waved back. The sweet scent of perfume filled their noses and a cheer erupted from the men.

"Major Peterson," The Captain saluted. "With General Lee's compliments." He smiled as his hand waved towards the wagons. "Sir, the General sends his regards as well as these lovely Southern Belles, a band and a wagon full of whiskey, beer, and food for you and your men. The south is grateful for what you did yesterday."

"Captain," Mark smiled back as he saluted. "On behalf of my officers and men please thank the General for his generosity." Mark smiled as he watched the Marines help the women from the wagons first. Each man found a companion leaving three to make their way to the medical tent to raise the spirits of the injured. The Marines quickly helped the seven members of the band from the wagon before carrying the food to the cook tent and the beverages to the center of camp. A quick table was created and the whiskey bottles emptied from the boxes and set on top. Two large casks of beer were set up next to the table as Corporal Engleman brought all the mugs from the cook tent and set them out to be filled. A beautiful blonde, with shoulder-length hair and a bright yellow dress, grabbed Corporal Engleman's arm. "I'll help you cook Corporal," She smiled as she spoke in a thick southern drawl. She led the blushing man to the cook tent swooning over him the whole distance.

Benches were brought from around the
camp and set up in a circle to create a
dance area as the band started to play. The
Marines had no idea how to dance with the
19th-century women, so they let the ladies
lead. Laughter erupted each time a Marine
tripped over his own feet as he tried to
woo the woman on his arm by dancing. The
Marines that were raised in the south had a
distinct advantage as they had learned how
to do some of the dances by holding their
mother's hands when they were young.

Three of the women walked toward the
command tent and were staring hard at the
three officers there. "Mark what would our
wives say about this?" Brian asked as he
smiled at the brunette in the purple dress.

"Well, technically Amy and I don't get
married for another 136 years," Mark
replied as he straightened his hair and
smiled at a fiery redhead with lust in her
eyes and a blue dress that emphasized her
bust line.

A woman with short brunette hair and a
big floppy pink hat that matched her dress
broke off from the trio and sat next to the
injured Lieutenant on the stump. She had a
small fan splayed in her hand that she
waved in front of her face. "Oh my, I hope
you're not in pain, lieutenant." Her
southern drawl disarmed the warrior in a
second.

"Well ma'am," Jerry started to speak
but was cut off instantly as she kissed him
on the mouth. The kiss lasted for 30

seconds before she pulled away and fanned herself again. "No ma'am, not in pain at all." He smiled back and leaned in for a second dose of her medicine. When he pulled away he spoke again, "Jerry Brown ma'am."

"Rebecca Frost, but you can call me nurse for now," her southern drawl and wide smile made the Marine blush as the nurse gave him another dose.

Brian and Mark laughed hard at the exchange before their escorts stepped in front of them. Names were exchanged and pleasantries offered. Everyone found their way to the drinks and the refreshments flowed all night. Over an hour had passed before anyone had seen Doug step from the cook tent. He asked for help and platters full of food were brought to the table for all to enjoy. Ham, sausages, mutton, and chicken along with vegetables, fruits and all manner of cakes and pies filled the table. Some drank, some ate and some disappeared for a time but everyone celebrated loudly. The band played for over an hour before finally taking a break and filling their bellies with food and drink. When they started round two a few brave, or drunk Marines took their ladies out to dance. The sun had set and the party carried on, music, laughter filling the air around the camp.

At midnight a half-detail of men relieved the sentries so they could partake in the revelry. Just after ten, someone commented on the disappearance of John Schanz and his lady, the big bear of a man

hard to miss even with all the
distractions. He reappeared just before
midnight, Dressed only in his linen union
suit, a bottle of whiskey in his hand and a
disheveled southern bell on his arm. A few
of her friends came over and pulled her
away and began to whisper to each other.
She retold the tale of new experiences,
even for her profession and the women all
gasped before turning to find their escorts
and disappear themselves for a while.

Chapter Twenty Eight

    Captain Pike walked out of his tent
into the bright rising sunlight. The camp
was a disaster area with men and women
lying everywhere. Sergeant Schanz laid face
down, the flap of his union suit open and
revealing his butt for the world to see.
His right arm draped over the half-naked
southern bell by his side. The thick
stockings and corset covering her while her
pink dress acted as a mattress for them
both.

    Brian shook the cobwebs from his head
as he stumbled to the command tent and
began making coffee. The smell of breakfast
hit his nose as he heard pans clanging in
the cook tent. The cold water he splashed
on his face helped wake him up and lowered
the volume of the brass band playing a tune
in his head.

    "Morning Brian," the captain turned to
see Mark walking up to the tent, the red-
haired maiden at his side with a wide smile
on her face.

    "Good Morning Captain," She spoke with
her deep southern drawl.

    "Where are my manners? Brian may I
introduce Miss Mary Murphy from the great

state of Virginia." He motioned to the young lady. "Mary may I introduce my second in command, Captain Brian Pike." He smiled as he gave her a wink.

"Pleasure is all mine ma'am," Brian said as he took her hand gently and kissed the bare skin on top as she blushed. "May I get you some coffee?"

"Why yes, yes please kind sir."

Brian handed the pair a mug and offered the chair to the lady. The trio sat and watched as the camp slowly came back to life. Mary told them how she grew up just outside the small town of Bracey, in southern Virginia. Her family owned a large plantation there and grew cotton and tobacco before the war. She lost a brother and two cousins to the north in the battle of Manassas. Her mother had died of consumption and her father went mad with all the grief. She left the farm 2 years before and found her way to Charlottesville. She had a job working in a school for a while but they let her go when all the boys went to war. She had to survive so she met up with a few of the women in the camp and they found a new way to make money. She was not the least bit embarrassed as she told the story to the two men. Mark reached over and put his hand on her knee as she spoke. She gave him a warm smile before taking another sip of the steaming coffee. "Well, this major showed up two days ago and handed us a stack of money and asked if we would host a party for the Heroes of Gettysburg."

Mark spit coffee out his nose. "The what?" he coughed out as he wiped the dark liquid from his face. Brian almost mimicked his friend as he watched the sight.

"That's what he said. He said the south would not have won that battle if not for you boys." She seemed proud to say the words. "Well, what is a good southern girl to do? We could not let our boys go without a celebration. So we loaded up in the wagons and headed here. We met up with the food and band and the second wagon of ladies and the rest is history."

Both men laughed at the last word. "Well yes, it was an epic shindig, my lady," Brian added with a tilt of the head and a salute with the coffee.

Corporal Engleman appeared with three plates stacked with food. "Breakfast?" he asked as Mary sat her cup on the table and picked up the fork offered to her.

"Oh my," she exclaimed. "I haven't had fresh eggs and bacon in months. Thank you, sir." She spoke without being able to look away from the plate. Lifting the piece of bacon to her nose she drew a deep breath and the men could almost see her mouth begin to water. She took a bite as she closed her eyes. A soft moan escaped her lips as she chewed the piece of heaven.

The tent grew quiet as the trio enjoyed the food. The men were happy that it helped with their minor hangovers. Men and women entered the cook tent as they made their way from around the camp. Every woman held fast to their soldier. They all had smiles and obviously had more fun than they had ever experienced before. Brian watched as he ate and thought about how much things would be different for them. The 19th-century woman having 21st-century sex, he couldn't help but smile at the thought.

Mark took Mary's empty plate and refilled it for her as Brian got a plate for his brunette date, Annabelle. "Morning Annabelle," Mary said as she dug into the second plate.

"Morning Mary," the lady smiled back before smelling the plate of food and digging in with gusto. "Oh my…bacon," Annabelle exclaimed with a broad smile.

"Well, life has no meaning without bacon ma'am." Brian laughed as he watched her put a whole piece in her mouth, her shoulders sinking low as she savored the flavor.

"You can say that again," She finally replied after she swallowed.

Men hurried through breakfast and gave their dates a kiss and promised they would be back before heading to relieve the night security so they could get some food, rest and company.

The abandoned women gathered near the campfire and whispered to each other about their special night as those who woke up alone joined their soldiers as they returned to camp. The day progressed calmly as men and women sat and told each other their stories. A few sat at the edge of the river, bare feet cooling off in the stream as the sun crawled higher in the sky.

Before noon the sentries announce riders were approaching. The marines started to head for their weapons until they saw the "Stars and Bars" flying over the horses as they approached.

Brian and Mark moved to meet them. The horses came to a stop and the Captain gave a salute from the horses back. "Major, General Lee requests your company at his command post, sir."

Both men noticed Sergeant Bill Sutton heading to saddle the horses. "Give us a few moments Captain and we will join you." Mark and Brian both headed off to get their uniforms on as the two officers looked at the women in the camp. Both knew that one hell of a party had taken place and they both smiled at each other.

Ten minutes later both officers were riding behind the guides with Sergeants Sutton and Schanz bringing up the rear. Brian laughed at the site of the big 6'5" marine on the horses back. "Damn John, you make that horse look small. Poor thing's gonna have a heart attack." All the men laughed loudly.

"Not my fault these horses are not adult size sir." Schanz fired back as he laughed along with them.

"May I ask a question sir?" the captain asked from the front.

"Uh oh," Mark thought to himself. "Of course Captain," he replied.

"Your weapons sir?" the man asked quizzically nodding to the pistols on the officer's belts and the rifles slung over the sergeant's backs. "Ain't ever seen the likes before."

"We have been trying to build weapons that would outshoot the Sharps and the Gatling gun. They seem to work pretty well, don't you think?" He turned and smiled at Schanz with a wink.

"They sure took the fight to the yankees, sir. Put the fear of God in some of us as well." The lieutenant riding up front spoke.

"Just glad we could make a difference," Brian added as the command tent came into view. General Lee had kept his post on the hilltop where General Meade surrendered. As the men approached the tents on the outskirts of the camp they were met with cheers. The soldiers ran to cheer the Marines as they waved their hats in the air. The Marines blushed as they nodded to the gathered soldiers.

The southern officers stepped outside the large tent as the riders approached. The men dismounted and the sergeants took the reins. Both officers approached the gathered generals and saluted crisply. "Major Peterson and Captain Pike reporting as ordered sir," Mark spoke proudly.

All the gathered generals returned the salute. "Welcome back gentleman," Lee spoke as he shook both man's hand. "Sorry to pull you both away from the party so soon." He fired off an evil grin. "I assume you and your men enjoyed themselves?" The gathered officers all smiled knowing what was sent as thanks.

"Yes sir General, Thank you from all of my men. That was more than generous." Mark replied with a smile of his own.

"Gentleman," Lee spoke in his command voice to the gather officers. "We have sent word to both the Union command staff as well as our own. Our scouts say that the Union Generals all dispatched riders at gallop towards Washington. It is safe to assume President Lincoln knows by now of our victory. President Davis has sent back word but it has yet to arrive. I'm not sure if they will believe what they are told even with the news from those soldiers that were able to escape." Brian shot a sideways glance to Mark knowing what was coming next. "I think we need to prove our capabilities one more time."

"General Lee I agree," Longstreet was the first to speak. "If we can show them

another decisive victory so quickly they
will have no choice but to surrender."

"Lee I concur. So, where do we strike
next? Major Peterson?"

"Sir, Our scouts report General Hooker
is about a 9 or 10-hour ride north of our
camp," Mark spoke matter of fact.

"Yes, our scouts say the same thing,"
Lee responded. "What are you thinking?"

"Sir I will send a squad of my
sharpshooters and cannon to his camp. I
will have them deploy outside their
shooting range on 2 different sides. Catch
them in a crossfire from so far out they
won't hear the shots till the bodies start
to fall. We can target their junior
officers and senior enlisted with our
rifles and their wagons and cannons with
our motors. Hit them quick and then
disappear before they can attempt a
counter-attack. If they stay in place we
hit them again the next morning and then
head back to our camp. This should scare
the hell out of them and they will have to
report this to Washington."

Lee took a drink from a coffee mug
that he picked up from the table behind
him. The gathered officers smiled at the
thought. General's Longstreet and Pickett
both smiled wide imagining the carnage they
would create, given their performance from
two days ago.

"Gentlemen," Lee finally spoke after 5 minutes of thought. "I approve of this battle plan. Have your men move out first thing in the morning. I will send scouts to your right flank to report directly to me on your progress. When your men return send me report on casualties and disposition of the Union force." Lee saluted to tell the men it was time to leave.

"Yes sir," both men saluted back before turning on their heels. Mark and Brian mounted their horses and headed back through the tents. Soldiers all tipped their hats to the Marines, a few reaching out for a handshake. When they left the camp and entered the tree line Mark looked to Brian, "What do you think Captain?"

"I like it. It will be a total surprise and raise all kinds of hell within their camp." Brian smiled. "Doc Brown made a comment to Jerry that fits well. "The futures not what it used to be."

"Amen," they heard Schanz reply from behind.

Chapter Twenty Nine

"Mr. President?" The well-dressed man walked into the cabinet room.

"Yes, Thompson?" Lincoln replied as the other men grew quiet.

"Sir, General Hooker is here to see you, sir. He says it is urgent."

"He is supposed to be in West Virginia?" Secretary of War Edward Stanton spoke to the man on his right.

"Show him in please," Lincoln spoke as a look of concern covered his face.

"Mr. President," Hooker saluted as he entered. "Gentleman," he nodded to the rest of the gathered men.

Lincoln stood and shook the man's hand before offering him a seat. "General I can only assume you are here to give us bad news. What do you have to report?"

"Gentleman, The division escorting me safely back to Washington to resign has been destroyed." The gathered cabinet members looked incredulously at the general. "Before you ask how I must say I am not completely sure myself. We heard of

the destruction at Gettysburg. My officers
and I were gathered to try and first figure
out how the South had created such weapons.
And second how to counter them." A butler
appeared and placed a glass of whiskey in
front of the general. "Thank you," He spoke
quickly before taking a sip and continuing.
"Suddenly things began to explode around
the camp. I had several officers killed in
minutes and never hearing the report of a
rifle. Ammo and supply wagons blew up
without hearing a single cannon. Some of
the men ran but most gathered weapons and
began to shoot in all directions. The
sergeants and officers tried to organize
the men but they were shot down quickly. I
ran outside the cabin we were using as a
command post and saw the confusion. Two of
my officer tents exploded with some junior
officers inside or nearby and they were all
killed instantly." Hooker paused to take
another swig from his glass. "Mr. President
the attack lasted for an hour. We never saw
a single enemy soldier or heard more than a
few dozen rifle shots before it stopped.
Just like that," he snapped his finger. "It
was done, sir. I looked around to find half
my camp burning or in pieces. I gathered
what officers I had left and given half
orders to organize the remaining men and
begin to break down and move the army. Sir
I am at less than half strength. I took
five officers and twenty men with me and we
rode hard for Washington." He finished the
whiskey in one last gulp as the butler
moved to refill his glass. The gathered men
sat silently for several minutes as
President Lincoln stroked his beard.

"General," the president finally spoke. "Can we defeat this new enemy?"

General Hooker stared at the brown liquor as he slowly swirled it in the glass. "No," he replied, the defeat obvious in his voice. "We don't even know how many of them there are. Or where they are at." The man paused in deep thought. "Maybe if we had the time to set up an ambush, but given their firepower it would have to be one heck of a big force." He paused again before his shoulders dropped. "So I am sorry sir but no, no we cannot beat them."

"Mr. President!" the cabinet members shouted all trying to voice an opinion.

"Mr. Stanton," Lincoln spoke, gaining control of the meeting.

"General Hooker, since when did you become one to give up so easily?" The Secretary of war asked.

"Mr. Stanton, I cannot and will not, give my men to die when it would be an obvious slaughter. Sir, I never once saw a flash from neither a weapon nor a soldier holding a weapon and they laid waste to my camp like it was made of match sticks. It is one thing to ask your men to stand in formation, in front of an enemy and fight when they can exchange ammunition. It is another to ask your men to form up not knowing where the enemy is and just take fire. Mr. President," Hooker turned to his commander in chief and swallowed the entire contents of his glass. "I had two of my senior officers killed by one shot in front of me. Their blood painted the side of the building I stood next to, yet I could not tell you where the shot came from or what fired it."

Secretary of State William Seward was the next to speak. "Gentlemen we have trusted General Hooker all this time, why is it so hard to believe him now." He looked to the men seated at the table. "Given what we were told about General Meade's defeat and with this new information, we have to ask ourselves if we wish to lose more of our countrymen in what has become an unwinnable situation." He motioned for the butler and a glass of whiskey appeared in front of him before the butler refilled the Generals glass.

"Mr. Seward, Let's say we surrender. What is the next step?" the president asked as he stood and began pacing at the end of the large mahogany table.

"First we would need General Hooker to contact General Lee and surrender to him. Next, you will need to send a letter to President Davis and ask what his terms are. I am guessing he will want the south."

"Mr. Seward is correct sir," Hooker interjected. All the South has wanted is to be left alone to live as they wish to."

"Mr. President, I suggest we offer those eleven states that succeeded to Mr. Davis." Edward Stanton spoke.

"Gentlemen, unfortunately, we are not in a position to suggest anything if we are surrendering." Hooker finally spoke with more confidence. "I will leave immediately for Gettysburg and surrender to General Lee. I will have riders send word to our troops that we are surrendered and to stop all hostilities."

"Agreed General," the president spoke; "I will also send word confirming this and order them to make immediately for the northern states. Admiral Welles?"

"Yes, Mr. President?" The secretary of the Navy snapped upright in his seat."

"Send word for all our ships to halt any activity in the southern waters and against southern cities and make for our own waters immediately."

"Yes Sir," the man replied. He quickly stood and walked from the room.

"General Hooker please leave immediately for Gettysburg. I will have a letter sent to President Davis within the hour. Also, gentlemen, I will need to make congress aware of the situation and our plans for the future. Harpers Ferry reported the defeat at Gettysburg in this morning's paper so this may not be as big a surprise as we think."

You may be right sir," Seward spoke, "the reporter was quite detailed about how one-sided the defeat was. That may play in our favor."

"Mr. Thompson!" Lincoln shouted as General Hooker made his way out the door.

"Yes, Mr. President?" The man spoke from the doorway.

"I need you to take a letter." Thompson removed his coat and sat in the chair left vacant by General Hooker.

"Mr. President, shall we leave you to it, sir?" Mr. Stanton asked.

"Gentlemen please remain. I wish to have your opinion on my words before sending." Lincoln gathered his thoughts as his secretary prepared his papers.

"To President William Davis, Confederate States of America.

Dear Sir,

I am writing to inform you that at this moment General U.S. Hooker is on his way to meet with your General Lee at Gettysburg. The purpose of this meeting is to discuss the terms of surrender of the Union army. We find the current situation untenable and no longer wish to give away the lives of any man, no matter the uniform to a lost cause.

Four score and seven years ago our fathers brought forth on this continent a new nation conceived in Liberty, and dedicated to the proposition that all men are created equal. We have been engaged in a great civil war, testing whether that nation or any nation so conceived can long endure.

The world will little note, nor remember the words I say here. With Malice towards none, with charity for all, with firmness in the right as God gives us to see the right. Let us strive to bind up our nations wounds, to care for his widows and orphans, to do all which may achieve and cherish a just and lasting peace, among ourselves, and with both our nations.

Signed on this day, July 14th, in the year of our lord 1863.

President Abraham Lincoln, United States of America"

The room was silent as Thompson set his pen down and stared at the president. After several moments Mr. Stanton spoke, "perfectly worded sir."

"I agree," the Secretary of State offered.

"Mr. Thompson, copy that and send it to President Davis by our fastest courier." Lincoln sat in his chair and let a long sigh escape his lips.

Chapter Thirty

It had been three days since his men returned from the attack on General Hooker's camp. The overwhelming success was described in detail upon their return along with the fact that Hooker had gathered a few men and high tailed it towards Washington.

Major Peterson looked out from his command tent and watched at what had almost become boredom for his marines. The daily routine had been made easier by their guests. Mark and Brian both agreed that, given the situation, why not let the men enjoy some female company. The women were in no hurry to leave as Mark overheard a few talking while the men were on mission. They were enjoying how the 21st-century man treated them differently than the 19th-century men would. Thank God none of the men tried to explain where they were truly from or they would have been deemed insane immediately.

"Rider approaching sir," a sentry yelled out and Mark looked to see the southern soldier slow from a gallop before he entered the camp. Brian and Mark walked from the tent to meet him.

"Message for Major Peterson with
General Lee's compliments," the soldier
saluted before handing Mark a yellowed
piece of paper. He turned and headed off
without another word.

Mark unfolded the paper and read it
quickly. "General Hooker and the north have
surrendered to General Lee at Gettysburg."

"Well, we guessed that would happen,
Mark." Brian offered with a smile. "Any
ideas what to do now?"

"None. The past really is dead I
guess. No idea where the world goes now.
General Lee wants us to report to his
command tomorrow morning. For now, pass the
word and see what the men think."

"Aye aye sir," Brian saluted and
walked towards a group gathered by a fire.

Mark knew everyone thought it was good
news by the way the women would throw their
arms around their man and hug him tight.
Brian was making his way through the camp
when he stopped in his tracks and looked
west. A huge thunderclap sounded as a storm
was brewing not far away. Mark sent word to
pull the sentry posts in since they would
not be able to see anything in a storm and
he preferred them close to camp. And since
the Union surrendered he need not worry
about an attack.

The dark clouds seemed to appear out
of nowhere as the storm built. Lightning
flashed across the sky and separated into

several fingers. The thunder followed immediately and hurt Mark's ears it felt so close. Brian shot through the opening of the tent, drenched by the rain that had started.

The marines all grabbed their women and pulled them into a tent. Three of the marines and their escorts stayed in the cook tent to avoid the drenching they would get trying to run across the camp to their tents. They held them close as the thunder assaulted their ears.

The inside of the tent grew bright as two bolts of lightning struck close by. The world went green as the tent shook from the wind and rain outside. Brian could see Mark trying to tell him something but between the rain and thunder, it was too loud to hear him. The air smelled like an electrical fire as lightning struck just outside the command tent and sent the two officers to the ground unconscious. The last thing Mark saw was a green glow and the grass smoking from the heat of the lightning.

Chapter Thirty One

Brian Pike awoke with a headache and a ringing in his ears. He sat up and shook his head to reset his equilibrium. When he finally could open his eyes he saw Mark prone a few feet away. The rising sun began to light up the tent. It took him a moment to realize that Mark's uniform was no longer a patch quilt of gray but now dark blue. The table was overturned and the map on the ground but the ground was dry. "How can that be after that rain?" he asked himself as he crawled to try and wake his commanding officer. "Mark," he shook the man.

It took a few moments but Mark replied with a grunt. Brian helped him sit up as Mark finally opened his eyes. "Holy hell, what a headache." He said in a small laugh. He stopped and stared at his XO. "Uh, Brian why is your uniform blue now?"

"I was going to ask you the same thing sir," Brian replied as he stood and helped Mark to his feet.

They both walked outside to find the layout of the camp had changed. The river that ran along the edge of the camp was gone. The medical tent had switched places with the cook tent. Corporal Engleman staggered out from the cook tent rubbing his head. His uniform had also become a patchwork of different shades of blue.

The men slowly began to exit their tents, all with the same look of confusion on their faces. A couple stopped and quickly looked back inside their tents. "Where did the ladies go?" He wondered out loud causing others to look around for the women they had spent the last ten days with.

Mark pulled a tarp off the weapons crates to the left of the command tent. "United States of America" had been painted on the top. "Well, Brian I think we have an answer." He pointed to the crate as Brian approached.

"Now when the hell are we?" Brian exclaimed as some of the men gathered. Brian turned and walked back into the command tent and returned with the map he found on the ground. "Well according to this we are Southeast of Power's Hill near Rock creek. That puts us maybe an hour march from Meade's HQ." Brian informed the Marines as he handed the map to Mark.

Sargent Schanz walked back to his tent and grabbed his rifle and backpack. He quickly went through the contents and announced "Sir, we have all the same equipment as before with minor changes to clothing. This all appears to be union issue now."

Corporal Engleman walked back from the cook tent, "Sir same with the food but it

is stamped U.S.A. and we have flour instead
of cornmeal."

"Ok, so whatever is doing this to us
decided to send us back again but to the
Union side I guess."

Lieutenant Jerry Brown walked out of
the medical tent. "Ok someone wants to tell
me how my wound healed overnight?" The
marines all turned to see him walking
without a limp and his uniform pants were
pristine and not cut open from when Doc
Brown sutured his leg. "Let me guess, we
are not in Kansas anymore?" He laughed
trying to lighten the mood.

"Sutton!" Mark bellowed as the man
stepped forward.

"SIR!"

"Grab a horse and ride northwest. If I
guess correctly you will find the Union
army not too far away." The thought was
punctuated by the sounds of cannon and
musket fire. "Try not to be seen but report
on the situation."

"Sir, riders approaching!" one of the
marines shouted as they all turned and
brought rifles up to the ready position.

"Weapons down," Brian ordered seeing
the blue coats of the riders and a general
insignia on the man in front. The men rode
up on the command tent.

"Who's in command here?" The general asked.

Mark made a quick decision and quickly rifled through his memory of the Union command. "I am sir, Major Mark Peterson, 149th New York under Brigadier General Geary Sir." Mark finished with a salute. "May I ask who you are please?"

"Brigadier General Williams, Major. What are you men doing here?"

"Sir, General Geary had me take my unit and move around behind the enemy lines and harass them. We left Culp's Hill mid-morning yesterday and destroyed a supply train meant for Ewell's Corp. We set up camp late last night with the intent of heading west this morning where my scouts tell me a large portion of the Confederate army is camped." Brian suppressed a smile as he heard the Major tell a convincing lie.

"That would not be a good idea, Major. ALL of Lee's army is there and we have word that 3 more Corp joined them late last night." The General looked at the gather soldiers for a moment. He didn't ask about the strange rifles a few carried but decided they all looked serious enough. "Major, leave your tents here but move your men to the northwest. Join Slocum's XII Corps on their right flank. He can use the extra men. Word has it the south has some secret unit they plan to send at us."

"Yes, sir!" Mark saluted.

"Make haste Major, the enemy could
attack at any time." The general ordered as
he turned his horse and he and his men rode
off.

The marines all stared at each other
as the silence around the camp became
deafening. Several minutes passed with the
sound of the occasional distant cannon
firing. "Ok marines, we have some serious
issues to address here," Brian said finally
breaking the silence.

"That's the understatement of the year
Captain," Sergant Schanz replied making the
men shake their heads.

"Well, we know this special unit is
us." Mark offered with no surprise. "The
general is putting us right across the
field from where we will be."

"So we changed history once, does this
mean we can change it back?" Jerry Brown
asked.

"Apparently something is giving us the
chance," Mark replied.

"Well lets "what if" this," Brian
offered. "So the North surrendered, America
was split into the U.S.A. and the C.S.A. We
have the Mexican-American war to fight,
World war one, which country fights for
which side? Does the south keep slavery?"

"Great question captain since even
General Longstreet thought they should have

freed the slaves before firing on Fort
Sumter." Lieutenant Brown offered.

"So we can only guess on the
possibilities of what we will do today if
we let our southern selves open fire." Mark
pondered out loud. The gathered marines let
the officers hold this discussion as they
were as clueless about what is right or
wrong here.

Brian looked at the gathered men for a
face. "Since Sargent Flint is not here we
can assume he shot his ancestor and
disappeared. So if we were to fire on
ourselves we would disappear as well and
keep the possible future from happening."

"I wonder if we go back to when we
should be if we disappear. Will I end up
back home with Lorrie?" Sutton asked,
making the men all drop the heads in the
thought of seeing their wives again. "I
didn't think that was possible so that's
why I didn't mind the last ten days of
female company." He smiled as a few other
marines' nodded agreement.

"Gentlemen, I can give you the same
speech as I did a few days ago about being
military men and having orders but this is
an even more bizarre situation than before.
If we shoot ourselves we have no idea what
will happen to us. Before we knew we would
fight and live in a different world. We had
the bravado and arrogance available to know
that we would decimate our enemy." Mark
paused as he looked into the faces of his
marines. "Now we are faced with our own

destruction to return to the world that we
grew up in. To return the world to the
history most of us studied. So we need to
decide and it must be unanimous."

"Sir?" Sargent Schanz raised a hand.
Mark nodded for the man to continue. "Sir,
I say we return things to the way they were
sir. We had a chance to live a dream of any
uniformed soldier, to fight in the "what
if" scenario most have talked about.
Doesn't matter if it's the Civil War or the
revolutionary war, we took our modern
weapons back in time and showed what could
happen. But, I think it's time to return to
our place in history and maybe return to
the lives and families we knew before."

The officers watched as all the men
bobbed their heads in agreement. "Marines,
what say you?" Mark asked in a subdued
voice. He smiled briefly as he remembered
the cheers from when he said this, what to
them, was a few days ago. "All those in
favor?"

"Aye!" was heard in unison.

"Opposed?" Mark asked only to hear
silence. "Gear up Marines. We move out in
ten." Mark ordered as the men dispersed.
"Well, Brian, what say you?"

"I agree fully Mark. We had our fun.
We answered the big question. Now I would
like to go home, if possible, to Ladonna
and the kids." Brian pulled his backpack on
and bent to gather his rifle. "You realize

we could be court-martialed right?" Brian
spoke without turning.

     "What in the hell are you talking
about Brian?" Mark stopped and stood to
hold his pack in his right hand.

     "We are about to shoot ourselves,
Mark. It's against the military code of
justice to commit suicide." Brian let go of
a belly laugh as Mark joined in.

     "You're an idiot Brian," He continued
to laugh as he grabbed his rifle and headed
out of the tent.

Chapter Thirty Two

        Mark pulled his pocket watch out
from his vest and noticed it was 10:45. His
men were lined up across the fence with the
mortars twenty yards behind. All his men
had confirmed the location of their
doppelganger. "Brian?"

        "Major?" Brian stood beside him with
his binoculars in hand.

        "If I remember correctly we had
Sargent Tyler shoot first with his .50
caliber?"

        "Yes sir I did," Tyler announced from
his perch ten feet to the officers left. "I
can see me sitting there with that cigar
you gave me."

        "Well, I guess now is a good a time as
any since your scheduled to shoot first in
15 minutes. Gentlemen," Mark spoke loudly
to his Marines. They all turned their
heads. "It has been a privilege and an
honor to serve with you. I hope to see you
again real soon. Sargent?" Mark turned and
looked at the sniper. "You may fire when
ready."

        Tyler brought the butt of his .50
caliber rifle to his shoulder and pulled it

tight. Mark stopped to shake Brian's hand.
Brian just smiled as the pair heard Tyler
click the safety off the big gun.

     Tyler had left the suppressor off his
rifle this time. He didn't need to hide the
report. He took aim at himself. The picture
of his face with a slight smile as he
enjoyed a cigar shook as the trigger
snapped clean like glass and the monster
rifle barked. The sounded echoed through
the valley.

     END.

ACKNOWLEDGEMENTS

To Michael Hall, whom I spent countless hours in an ambuance discussing and deciding the basic concepts of the book. All stemming from his time as a special forces medic.

To Brian Pike and Mark Peterson, who without their help the military side of this book would have been a disaster. Thank you both for the hours of conversation, ideas and encouragement.

To Nikcyi Cifani, for encouraging me; your enthusiasm has grown past the undead and has kept me writing. Of course the occasional threat of great bodily harm from your axe helps also.

To my kids, Jerry and Katie for their love and support.

To my Mother, she listened to me vent without having a clue what I was venting about. Also for the constant support and occasional dinner.

To Rebecca Kaiser, for her awesome cover art. You made my vision become reality.

To Michelle and Sean, My editors for their hard work and dealing with all the questions and issue of post-production.

If I forgot anyone please understand it is not intentional. I love all my friends that helped make this possible!